A Tale of Truths

Berit Ellingsen

"*A Tale of Truths* reads like a campfire tale, a bedtime story adventure, a road trip yarn spun to wile the hours. It begins with an elf shaped from the sea shore, and quickly fills with extraordinary thieves, a cat that is horses, and a journey by hearse through a sentient forest. What we have here is quirky unpredictable playfulness let to run rampant."

–C. S. E. Cooney

"Berit Ellingsen's *A Tale of Truths* is a seamless and beguiling act of world-building as storytelling, a joyous celebration of humanity's addiction to both rational and magical reasons for the worlds we perceive. A delightfully curious fantasy, in the truest sense."

–Indra Das

Cover art and design by Bizhan Khodabandeh

Rosarium Publishing
P.O. Box 544
Greenbelt, MD 20768-0544

www.rosariumpublishing.com

A Tale of Truths

Berit Ellingsen

For Dotty and Chloe

deeply loved and sorely missed

One
The Cold Coast

THE COAST WAS COLD AND HAGGARD and at the edge of the wide white wastes of the north. In the winter storms from those wastes reached down to the coast with their icy hands, freezing the sea to ice. In the fall the sun's rays slanted at such a low angle it was unable to transfer any warmth, and long waves crashed onto the shore from storms far out in the ocean. But in the spring the bright sun turned the mountains golden, and the peaks and the waves played hosts for enormous flocks of birds that returned from friendlier southern shores. The birds came to feed in the cold sea and rear their young in the cliffs above it. Then the pufflings and auklings and cormorant chicks only needed a small nudge to get out of the nest and into the waves when they were ready to swim. At the height of summer, the sun never fell beneath the horizon, and cotton grass and tiny white orchids grew at the massive feet of the mountains. Eider ducks lined their burrows with soft down, and summer-gray foxes lurked in the grass to catch themselves a bird or two. Thus, the frigid coast was not entirely hostile to its inhabitants and guests and in many ways was more generous than places farther south, but it was nevertheless a demanding place to live.

***

THE ELF HAD watched the coast for many seasons, seen the sea ice come and go, watched thickly furred bumblebees buzz over the grass in the spring and the pufflings and auklings and cormorant chicks flap their wings desperately before they tumbled into the sea from the cliffs. The elf didn't know where he had been before he came to the cold coast. When he cast his mind back into the past he had always been there, watching the wind and the sea and the mountains. Plants and animals had come and gone, the coast line frozen and melted and frozen again. He began to wonder what the wind and the sea and the mountains would feel like, their scent and texture and taste. And the desire to experience it for himself came to him suddenly with surprising urgency. After the wish for experience first appeared, being and watching was no longer enough. The desire had been born and with it an expectation of pleasure that was almost painful in its intensity and an anticipation of pain that was almost as joyful. Once awakened, the yearning for experience would not let itself be set aside or ignored or forgotten. It reappeared in the elf's mind again and again until he finally let go and allowed himself to fall into the longing.

From the gleam of the stars on black winter nights, the salty waves in the ocean, the massive peaks along the coast, and the breeze that moved as quick as thought, the elf created a slim body and narrow face with long eyes and hair until he appeared on the stripe of wet sand that lay between the ocean and the grass. The cold water that licked his feet burned his skin, and the gale that howled into his tapering ears stung sharply; but the grass trembled, and the surf breathed onto the sand in rhythm with his heart. The elf waded ashore. Despite the sunny autumn day, the coast felt just as he had expected; chilly, remote, and demanding. It was beautiful—the same way a strong gust of wind takes your breath away and winter cold eats into your nails. He smiled. It was as good a place to start as any.

***

THE ELF KNELT and placed a palm on the small, round pebbles at the high-water mark. The stones had been polished by the sea, each holding their own color; brown, black, white, orange, pink. Among the stones, tufts of gray eiderdown had been caught. From the smoothness of the pebbles and the softness of the eiderdown, he fashioned warm, gray robes. Finally, the elf wreathed some tiny orchids into his hair.

A bit farther up on the beach stood an old trapper's hut weathered gray by the elements. In its shadow a small gray creature watched the elf from the grass. He could feel the other being's pale green, slitted eyes on him, observing him with fear, curiosity, and a tiny expectation in its cold, hungry body. The elf pulled his gray robes close and squatted on the sand. A potential companion. That could come in handy.

"Here, little friend," the elf said and held out his hand. The green eyes bobbed, following his hand intently. What did the gray cat want the most? Food? Water? It turned out not to be what the elf expected. The cat approached him cautiously on tense paws, hoping that he was friendly and would not chase her away. When the elf neither attacked nor grasped at her the cat sniffed his hands for a little while, then pushed her head against them to make him pet her, even food forgotten in the hope of love. The cat was small but strong with large round eyes and a short, dense coat that was surprisingly smooth for having lived on her own since harvest time.

The elf fed the cat fresh water and eider eggs, then the cat slept for a long time in his lap while he sat cross-legged in the grass and watched the surf roll onto the shore. When the elf and the cat awoke the brief hurried days of the north had grown dark.

"The sun has already turned toward winter," the cat meowed.

The elf nodded at her. "Don't worry. It will return soon."

The cat slung her short tail around the elf's ankle, purred, and pushed at his hands.

"Would you like to come with me?" the elf said. "I will

make certain you are loved and warm and fed, but then you have to do something for me."

"Of course," the cat purred. "I knew you'd ask."

The elf smiled.

"What is it that you want me to do?" the cat said.

"I want to go inland, but for that to happen we need to move faster."

The cat looked up at him, her green eyes glittering. "I guess it doesn't matter what I say," she meowed. "Just don't turn me into a dog."

Then she stood in front of him, as gray as before, but many times larger with black mane and tail and hooves and a proud round neck with only her green, narrow pupils revealing her true feline nature.

"Oh, a horse," the cat neighed. "And it's me."

THEY SHARED A meal together of fresh water from a stream, eider bird yolk from the burrows, and wild garlic from the meadow before they set off toward the mountains. The cat ran hither and yon like a kitten over the grass and kicked her hind legs every time the cold marsh water touched her hooves. The elf had neither saddle nor reins and could only clutch the long mane every time the cat reared. A small but very angry rodent ran up from its burrow in the wet grass, shouting at them. Immediately, the cat jumped high into the air and landed with sudden crushing impunity on the rodent. Then she beheaded and de-haired it with her dull horse teeth while she whinnied impatiently and scratched at the prey with her black hooves. The elf could not help but laugh and let the cat eat her prey as consolation for having such a new and foreign body.

Out of the cold, cloudberry-filled marshes, they spotted tall, narrow slits in the looming mountain sides. These were passes leading inland away from the coast and the surf and the wind. The elf hesitated. Did he really want to leave the open land for the forests? But then he remembered that he had the coast's salty water in his blood, its clear star light in his eyes, its mountains in his bones, and in his mind, the swiftness of its ever-moving wind. The cat had eiderdown in her mane and flowering grass straws curled about her ears. They would never leave the coast no matter where they went.

"Are you ready?" the elf asked the cat and led her toward the narrow opening in the mountain. The peak looked as if it reached the moon. Giving no reply, the cat reared up, galloped toward the pass with mud and peat flying from her hooves, and leapt into the pass.

Two
A System of Spheres

WALLS OF STONE LOOMED ABOVE THE elf and the cat with less distance than a person's height separating the two sides. In the darkness the elf couldn't see where the walls ended, but far above them white stars glittered in the narrow gap. The walls were so tall and so close it felt like they curved in on them. However, the walls were not blank. Their faces held horizontal lines and layers that varied in breadth from the thickness of a finger to heights larger than the trapper hut on the beach. These strata followed the pass along its entire length, and the number of them was in the thousands. Each layer had a color slightly different from that above and below in shades of black, brown, yellow, gray, orange, rust, and even purple. It was as if time had frozen in intervals and accreted layer by layer until the rock face reached higher than the eye could see.

At first the cat ran and jumped and made a few high-pitched whinnies when she tried to meow. After a while she slowed down to a trot, but that made the elf on her back bounce annoyingly. So she slowed to a brisk walk. The elf held out his arms so he could touch both walls of the pass with his fingers.

"What are you doing?" the cat whinnied.

"Examining," the elf said while he continued to trace the strata with his hands. It was like reading the passage of time. Countless sunsets and dawns had fallen and risen over the stone. Perhaps the pass had been forgotten by time and remained frozen outside of it. Or maybe it sat at the heart of time itself where all timelines converged. The elf kept his fingers on the stone until his skin turned blistered and raw.

THEY TRAVELED THROUGH the pass for a long while. Several times the elf asked the cat if she were tired and wanted to rest. To his surprise the cat only whinnied at him, blew air out her nostrils, and continued. She was more suited as a horse than he had thought a cat would ever be.

"Look! It's getting brighter," the cat neighed, waking the elf from his sleep where he was resting against her warm, strong neck. Yellow light shone on the upper sections of the pass. Now the walls were smooth and gray and vertical, not leaning inward as earlier. The cat's hooves clattered against the sand. No, not sand. Stones, cobblestones, each the size of a palm, laid out in an arching pattern on the ground. A shadow passed overhead, momentarily blocking out the light. The elf glanced up. An oblong box of some kind attached to the bottom ledge of a window. The walls on both sides held windows and ledges. The elf grinned. Now the pass was a narrow alley between two buildings in a city.

The alley ended in a gap almost as tall and thin as the entrance far behind them on the coast.

"What is that?" the cat asked.

"Have you been to a city before?" the elf replied. He was feeling a little apprehensive. The sound of many people walking, running, yelling, shouting in the morning sun reached them. The cat shook her elegant head and long black mane.

"No, I was born on the coast and lived there all my life. Have you been to the city before?"

"I haven't," the elf admitted.

The alley opened up to a large open space, a square lined with broad tenement buildings with green-shuttered windows and multitudes of narrow doors. Their ground floors housed restaurants and cafes and bakeries with small tables and narrow wooden chairs placed outside them. The seats were already occupied by women in long dresses and with long hair piled high beneath wide hats and fabric flowers and jeweled pins to keep the hats to the hair. Men in wide-sleeved coats with short pantaloons and bulging ankles also sat around the tables. The fine men and women sipped their sweet morning tea and nodded at acquaintances and neighbors who passed by their tables.

"Good morning!"

"Indeed, a lovely morning!"

It was the beginning of the day, and the city was waking up. Its inhabitants were having breakfast, feeding children, cats, and dogs; doing laundry; pumping water; unlocking workshops; opening stores; going to school; starting the day's work. The elf and the cat continued past the cafes and restaurants toward the tall steeple-roofed church at the end of the plaza. Above the arched entrance sat an enormous circular stained glass window in crimson and white with black lead edging. The rays of the autumnal morning sun blazed in the glass.

"How dramatic," the cat commented.

"Try not to relieve yourself here on the square among all these people," the elf replied.

"So you don't have to sweep it up, you mean? You should have thought of that before you turned me into a ..." meowed the cat, now possessing her original form. The elf bent down and hoisted the cat up on his shoulders.

There was a crowd assembled in front of the church, and it was growing quickly. The throng shouted and laughed, which made the cat nervous, so she meowed a little under her breath; but something was about to happen, and curiosity dictated that they stay. The crowd was staring up at the church tower above the beautifully nested arches of the entrance. Slowly and carefully, a strange contraption was lowered from the eaves to below the stained glass window. The mechanism was topped by a half-dome lined on the inner surface with cobalt enamel. Hundreds of tiny star-shaped openings had been cut into the dome, creating the backdrop of a starry sky beneath which sat a multitude of horizontally placed cogs of brass. Each cogwheel increased in diameter from the centermost to the most peripheral and carried an orb at the end of a metal stick. In the middle of the spheres hung a large ball of polished gold.

The elf and cat were soon surrounded by people who jostled and elbowed each other to get a better view of the contraption. The elf stood on his toes and stretched his neck to see better. There was something strangely familiar about the display like something he had seen in a dream full of certainty and purpose and forgotten upon awakening.

"What's that?" asked the cat. She dug her claws into the elf's long robes while she sniffed the air and grinned oddly in order to catch olfactory clues about the strange contraption.

"I'm not sure," the elf admitted. "I think I know what it is, but I can't say what it's called or how it works."

"Then we're just as far from the answer as before," scoffed the cat.

***

"LADIES AND GENTLEMEN!" a voice, tinny from being amplified by a metal cone, was heard above the crowd. "Join in the most important debate of our day!

"Does the burning sun and the lofty planets in the firmament follow the Earth like an obedient lap dog, or do we and all the other worlds in the heavens circle the sun? In other and perhaps simpler words, are we the center of the universe or does everything, for unknown reasons, revolve around the sun? In the final instance it will be you, the public, who will decide the outcome of this most important philosophical debate! Do not just leave it up to the scholars and the academics. Make the decision for yourselves!"

The elf placed his right hand over his mouth in a pondering gesture. He knew he should know the right answer to this riddle. But now he wasn't certain. The loud, jostling crowd was distracting him too much. "Oh, I know the answer to this already," the elf muttered in frustration.

"Really?" meowed the cat with feline confidence. "What a stupid question. Everyone knows the sun and the Earth are falling heedlessly through the darkness. Sometimes the sun is falling faster than the Earth, other times the Earth is going down first. That's why we have nights and days."

"Hmph," the elf replied. "Let's hear what the real answer is from this demonstration."

THE MORNING SUN glittered in the brass wheels and golden ball of polished smooth crystal in the middle of the display. But for a while nothing happened.

"What's taking so long?" an elderly man behind them asked.

"I need to get home with these before they hatch," a young woman with a basket full of large goose eggs said to her companion.

The cat dug her claws into the elf's shoulder and yawned. "Yes, what's the delay?" she meowed. "Perhaps they forgot to oil the joints of the contraption, and now it's stuck! Or it's turned out that the sun does fall through the darkness after the Earth and the model is no longer valid?" She made a strange hiccupping noise which the elf realized was cat laughter.

"Shh," he said. "The quiet before things begin is the best part. It really says everything that it is possible to truly say about any subject."

"But it's not silent here at all!" the cat protested and laughed again.

"That's because you're not listening close enough," the elf replied.

The cat buried her claws into the elf's skin again when suddenly the half-dome that hung above the contraption turned a little to block out the direct light from the sun. This put the rest of the display in shadow while the tiny openings in the cobalt enamel glittered with light like stars. Suddenly a yellow flame appeared on a cord beneath the cog wheels close to the ground. The fire rushed up along the cord and into the golden sphere, which burst into orange and yellow flames. The crowd shouted and screamed. Now all eyes were on the display.

THE THIRD ORB from the burning ball had been made of lapis lazuli and inlaid with continents of gold. Now it jerked into motion and moved a little forward, then a notch back, before it slowly started to turn on its own axis.

"The Earth!" the voice from the church tower began.

The crowd fell silent.

"The Earth!"

The elf laughed in excitement.

"The Earth has day and night, sunsets and sunrises, because it turns on itself, leaving one part in the light of the sun and the other in shade." As the blue orb revolved, the side facing the burning ball in the middle was lit up and the other half lay in relative darkness. As it spun slowly, the half that had been in light fell into shadow and the side that had been shaded by darkness moved into light.

This sight made the crowd yell various vowels. The cat's eyes turned round and dark. She sat completely still on the elf's shoulder, her whiskers turned forward and vibrating with tension. Her eyes were so large that the elf could now look through her eyeballs from the side and out on the world through her eyes. This made the elf smile. He had gotten a glimpse of how the cat viewed the world.

In the display a small silver orb attached to the lapis sphere began to move. It did not move on its own axis but began to circle the blue orb in a tight circumference around the blue planet, turning in and out of the shadow of the blue orb from the flame in the middle.

"Then we have the moon," the voice continued. "A world much smaller than ours, which looks to be waxing and waning as the month progresses while it pulls and pushes the oceans in its invisible wake across the sky."

The cat nodded in agreement. She had seen the high tide and the low tide at the coast and the silver light from the moon on the mountains. When the moon was hidden the darkness had been almost palpable while she hunted soundlessly in the thick grass by the beach.

In the display the Earth turned toward night and day while the moon encircled it. But then that entire part of the contraption—the blue orb and the tiny silver sphere that was attached to it—started to move, too! Together they moved much slower on their course around the flames than either the moon was moving around the Earth and the Earth was turning on its own axis. They did not move in a random fashion. Rather, they followed a slow, pondering, but complete course around the burning orb in the middle. It took a while before the crowd discovered that because not everyone had the patience to wait till the pair of orbs had moved an entire revolution around the fire. When other viewers pointed it out, however, there was more shouting and exclaiming.

"The moon is our companion, our satellite!" continued the voice from the tower. "It circles our planet once a month. But as our satellite encircles us, so do we circumnavigate another heavenly body together with the moon. That is the sun!"

Now it was clear for everyone that the blue orb, along with its small grey companion, was circling the still burning golden ball.

"We are not really falling through the sky but constantly hunting the sun!" yelled the cat. "Now I see it all!"

The elf looked at her. There was apparently an epiphany happening in the cat's mind. She was so excited that she clattered her teeth together in the same way she did when she severed the neck bones of her prey or when she saw birds pass overhead and could not reach them.

"BUT THAT IS not everything!" announced the voice. "Because we are not alone! There are many other worlds in the firmament! Closest to the sun there is Mercurius!"

A tiny odd-looking ball of pockmarked white gold started spinning and moving on a small gear close to the lit orb in the middle. It circled so close to the flames that they occasionally licked its surface, dusting the white gold with soot.

"Then we have Venusius, our southern neighbor!" A modest globe between the small pockmarked one and the blue started on its cogwheel revolutions. It was made from pale yellow electrum and was of the same size as the blue orb but moved a little faster around the sun. "We see this planet most clearly on winter dusks and autumn mornings such as now," the voice continued. "It looks like a star in the heavens. Yet it is not a star—but a planet like ours. It has no fire like the sun, only clouds, which makes it look faintly golden," explained the voice.

The cat shook her head. "Venusius is a star," she whispered. "I have seen it myself countless times on the beach at home. It shines like a star and glitters like one. Therefore, it is a star."

"Our neighbor to the immediate north is Ares, the planet of the god of war, but now fortunately placated," continued the voice. A golden sphere the color of salmon flesh dusted with silver on the poles started to move on the wheel outside the blue orb. This globe was smaller than the blue one. Its path around the sun was almost twice as large as the blue planet's.

"We are not finished yet!" said the voice. "Encircling the sun far beyond Ares, at a distance from us we can hardly imagine, is the planet Jovius." This was represented by a banded agate orb at least five times the size of the blue globe. The wheel this planet followed around the sun was longer than a man's arm, and the globe spun so slowly it first looked as if it did not spin at all. In the agate the mineral had been divided into parallel belts of different colors ranging from taupe to orange. On one side between the equator and the southern pole sat a red blotch like an evil eye.

"This is a planet many times larger than our own," boomed the voice. "Hundreds of our little blue world would fit inside Jovius if that were possible. And that might happen since Jovius consists mainly of gases."

Upon hearing the alien nature and almost forbidding knowledge of the planets, the limits of the imagination of many in the audience had been reached and rudely crossed, causing the rest of the organism to swoon to the ground. These hapless audience members were aided by their companions and woken up or escorted to the cafes and restaurants nearby for a glass of water and maybe something more invigorating. On the elf's shoulder the cat was swaying, too, the limits of feline ken also about to be reached.

"But have no worries, ladies and gentlemen!" the voice reassured. "Although the next planet is even more exotic and alien than Jovius and makes even larger demands on your nervous systems to imagine, we have finally come to the last of the planets in our solar system!"

A sigh went through the throng. More than a few people visibly steeled themselves against the strangeness of what they were about to hear.

"Saturnus is almost as large as Jovius. It too consists mainly of gases like our air, and it is blue like the oceans. It has several strange rings around it—like belts. No one knows what these are. Saturnus is so far away from us and the sun that one of its revolutions takes half a lifetime to achieve. And it can only be seen in the strongest of telecopes. But however strange and distant these other worlds are, they, like us, must follow the sun! This orb was almost as large as the previous one but made from lilac-yellow jadeite. Surrounding it was a narrow silver band that sat at a slight angle to the orb's equatorial plane. Its cogwheel was the largest and most distant from the central orb in the mechanism.

Upon witnessing this extraordinarily alien world, the crowd gasped again. Even a few young, healthy-looking people fainted and had to be carried away. The cat was whipping her tail against the elf's head. He let her, as he didn't want to interrupt her thinking.

"Merciful cat-hood!" she finally meowed and fell into a soft grey heap. The unconscious feline slid down into his arms where she was cradled warmly until she woke up again.

Three
The Equipage

Then the lecture was over. The moving wheels stopped, and the fire in the burning glass globe went out. People began to disperse. Yet their voices were still loud from excitement over the display.

"That was an original idea, but I'm not sure if I believe it," someone said.

"Everyone can see for themselves that the sun follows the Earth and not the other way around," said another.

"I, for one, believe the Earth revolves around the sun but not that there are so many planets outside of ours."

The viewpoints and comments were as many as there had been individuals in the throng.

AS REFRESHING AS the new perspective the lecture had described was, the elf was more curious about the idea itself, what its foundations were, and who it had come to. There was apparently more at work behind it than had been presented at the lecture. How had the creator of the display found out what the other planets looked like and at what speeds they orbited the sun? Not to mention what elements they were made from and what colors they possessed. Thus, the elf remained on the square close to the church door and the planetary display to see if anyone and in which case who came to dismantle it.

After a short while a teenaged girl in an acolyte's tan robes exited a side door from the church. She carried a tall stepladder under her arm, then placed it under the fire orb, climbed up, and spread out a thick blanket to cover the smoldering golden orb with.

"Careful, Alexandra. Smother, but don't rub the wick of the sun or it won't light up for our next presentation," a familiar voice said.

FROM HIS TABLE at the cafe closest to the church, the elf stretched his neck to see who was speaking. He recognized the voice as the same that had spoken in the lecture. An elderly woman with gray hair tied up into a large wobbly bun at the top of her head stood in the doorway. She was dressed in a long black robe that carried a bristling white collar. On the bridge of her nose sat two crescent-shaped lenses in golden frames. She must be the inventor of the fantastic display since she was worried about the model of the sun, the elf thought. And judging from her voice and inflection, she must be the lecturer as well. Was she perhaps also the proprietor of the ideas presented therein?

"Careful, careful." The old woman shuffled out from the door toward the stepladder and the girl with arms outstretched. "Let me do it, Alexandra."

"No, no, I'm fine!" said the girl, glancing down at the old woman. "Let me just shut the latch and I'm ready." The old woman nevertheless closed in on the ladder while she squinted up at the enamel orbs.

Yet another person emerged from the doorway, a middle-aged man dressed in a simple brown robe. His bald pate shone even in the overcast midday sun.

"Dame Logan, Alexandra, is everything going well? I'd rather avoid a near accident like last time we dismantled the model."

The girl dropped her arms to her sides and faced the monk directly.

"I'm fine, I'm fine, just give me some time."

The monk looked like he wanted to reply in kind but stopped himself. The girl returned to her work.

"Dame Logan, may I have a word with you?"

"Yes, yes." The old woman moved closer to the monk.

THE ELF SIPPED his lukewarm tea while watching the three people. It was like a little play, and it was amusing to guess the relationship between the three by the way they interacted with one other. Were they perhaps mother superior, monk, and novice, or madam, butler, and maid, or grandmother, son, and granddaughter?

When the old woman moved back to the doorway it grew difficult to hear what she said. The elf directed a small breeze toward him so he could hear their words on the wind.

"Dame Logan," said the monk. "I appreciate your taking the time and inventiveness of presenting your research here for the general public. But I'm afraid that my superiors don't wish to let the display remain, in particular with the winter celebrations closing in. The brothers feel that the display is not in the right spirit of the festivities."

"But I need to present the ideas to the public several times more to have any chance of applying for a lecture at the academy," the old woman said.

"I regret this terribly, of course, since I was the one allowing you to have the presentations in the first place," the middle-aged man added.

"I knew it," the old woman replied. "I knew your superiors would not like my ideas, no matter how well researched they were."

"Well, they are not scientists themselves, Dame Logan ..." said the monk.

"But it took days to set the display up!" yelled the girl on the stepladder. "Now you're asking an old woman to dismantle it after just one demonstration?"

"Yes. I know, I know. I'm truly sorry." The monk looked a little more hunched than before. "I do think the audience quite enjoyed the presentation, though, don't you?"

The youth turned back to the model with an exasperated sound and continued her work of teasing the remaining burned rags out of the small opening at the bottom of the golden orb.

"The girl is right," the old woman said. "We just set the display up, and it took us a lot of time. Can't it at least stay till tomorrow and another presentation?"

The monk nodded. "All right. I'll ask the brothers. But

please be ready to remove the display tomorrow afternoon. Besides, I'm sure you don't want snow on that expensive enamel hood."

"You do not really believe we will have snow yet?" the old woman asked and looked at the monk. The man raised his hand in a calming gesture and retreated back into the church.

THE GIRL ON the stepladder jumped down on the cobbles and began folding the stepladder flat.

"Don't worry, grandmother," she said. "We should just go directly to Spiral and hold the presentations there instead."

THE ELF PUT a few of the metal pieces that people liked to receive as payment on the table where he was sitting, picked up the still sleeping cat, and left his seat.

"Madam lecturer?" the elf asked and bowed to the old woman in black.

She turned and gave him such a searing gaze over the crescent-shaped lenses of her spectacles that the elf had to brace himself not to shrink back. "Who is asking?" she said.

Ignoring the curt welcome, the elf continued, "An elf of the northern shores." He bowed once more—more elaborately this time.

"Master Elf," the old woman said and made the tiniest of dips with her head in greeting. "I'm Dame Logan: scientist, inventor, and lecturer. Why are you calling upon me?"

The elf swallowed. No chance to beat about the bush here. "I was very impressed by the novelty and eloquence of your lecture," he began. "And I wanted to know if you would be so kind as to reveal more about the idea to an eager student? However brief and pithy. "

The old woman gave him another razor glance over her spectacles. "You mean the basis for my argumentation?" she said.

"Yes."

The scientist's eyes flared, but her frown was still in place. "Do you have any knowledge of science?"

"No formal one," admitted the elf, "but a strong interest. In the stars, in particular."

The scientist's face fell, and she sighed. "It's too long and complicated. It would only bore you."

The elf looked down, trying to find other entryways to the answers he wanted. "Could you at least reveal where you got the idea for the sun-centered system?" the elf added quickly. Perhaps if he were fast enough the old woman would reply out of pure eagerness before she had a chance to reconsider and evade the question.

But the old woman did not hesitate. "Why on Earth would you want to know that? Are you a servant of one of my detractors?"

The elf quickly shook his head. "No, I'm merely a fascinated member of the public and curious as to whether you will bring the lecture to other towns such as Spiral?"

At that the old woman visibly startled. Her granddaughter, who had remained in the background during the conversation, now looked at him with open curiosity.

"You hail from Spiral?" said the girl. Her grandmother now regarded the elf a tad milder.

The elf quickly evaded the question as he didn't quite have the gall to lie to the old woman's face. Instead, he said, "If you desire help to transport the display to Spiral, I have a strong, reliable horse.

"Perhaps," said the scientist with regained composure. "I may wish to hold a lecture there at a later point in time."

"He has a horse and carriage, momo," said the girl. "And we have to leave tomorrow. Say yes."

"All right," said the old woman. "If you are really serious about this, Master Elf, you may help bring the display to

Spiral. As payment, I shall tell you the basis for my arguments on the way."

"It will be my great honor and pleasure!" said the elf and wondered if he should reach for the scientist's hand to kiss it, but he thought it best not to. "When do you require the transport?"

The scientist thought for a moment. "Meet me here at noon tomorrow," she finally said. "We shall remove the display and prepare it for transport to Spiral. I do hope you have a carriage as the display is too wide for horses and we do not own any."

"The girl and you?" the elf asked.

The scientist nodded. "Yes, she is my assistant and noble heir."

"I'm looking forward to it, Madam Logan, and will procure a carriage," said the elf.

"Until tomorrow then," the scientist said, looking at the elf with a clear expectation that he would be gone from her sight.

"Farewell," the elf said and bowed one last time to the scientist.

"I HEARD THAT," said the cat. "You have neither horse nor carriage. And do you even know where Spiral is?"

"I have a horse," the elf said and grinned. "I just need a carriage. And Spiral. Let me think." The elf closed his eyes, wet his index finger, and held it up in the air. "Spiral is over there through the forest to the south. I can feel it."

The cat said nothing and started to wash herself.

RESOLUTELY, THE ELF stood and crossed the cobbles. At the end of the square, he ducked inside a small shop that lay half a floor below the ground, its narrow windows peering out at the shoes and ankles that passed by outside. The shop sold masks in bright colors decorated with silk, velvet, crystals, pearls, sequins, beads, gold leaf, brass, and semi-precious minerals. Some of them would cover half the wearer's head with strutting feathers and tufts of tulle and were so heavy they had to be held by a long stick in front of the face. Others only disguised the eyes, nose, and cheeks and were worn by thin strings attached to the sides of the mask and tied behind the head.

When the elf saw the masks shining and glittering with gems and beads and pearls he had to stand still for a moment to take in the display of dizzying colors, gleaming decoration, and eyeless faces. A small bell above the door rang. By a narrow desk on the floor three steps down, the owner of the store, a tall man with small round glasses perched on the tip of his nose and a pronounced belly covered in a brown leather apron, smiled at them.

"Get inside and close the door," the cat said. "You're letting all the heat out."

The elf woke from his reverie. "Oh, so sorry," he said and nodded to the shop's proprietor.

"Good afternoon, sir," said the pot-bellied man. "We have masks in all shapes and colors for all occasions. We even have simple white masks and sell beads by the half dozen for your decorating pleasures."

The elf held up his hand. "No, no. I already possess a very elaborate mask," he said. "I only need to know where the nearest carriage maker is."

The store proprietor pushed the glasses back up onto the bridge of his nose.

"Bartolomeo's makes carriages for the clergy. And a few other things. They're two canals east of here, just across the bridges. I fear they might be the only carriage maker for a good while."

"Really?" said the elf and headed for the door.

"Didn't you see all the canals on the other side of the square?" the cat said. "They probably only use boats here."

"What?" said the elf. "Only boats?"

"That's right," said the mask maker. "There are only a few horses in town and even fewer carriages. Boating on the canals is much faster than steering horses and carriages through the narrow alleys and bridges."

"How can a carriage maker survive in this city then?" the elf wondered.

The mask maker laughed. "Bartolomeo's a boat maker. But when the clergy needs a new carriage they convert a craft into a small hearse."

"A hearse?" the elf said. This was unexpected, yet useful news.

"They're the only ones in Canal to need a carriage, to transport the dead from the city and across the causeway to the mainland for burial. There is no room in Canal for graves, so the dead have to be consecrated in the churches in town."

"In that case," said the elf, "I'd better be on my way. Thank you for the directions and information." He waved his hand in the approximation of a small bow and slipped out the door under the dinging of the bell.

"Dear gods," sighed the cat.

AFTER SOME TIME'S fruitless search, crossing the wrong canals or entering the wrong side streets and then having to retrace their steps, the elf and the cat finally found the boat maker's workshop. It occupied a small part of the canal, where the water was kept away by an iron sluice, creating a dry dock and courtyard for the workshop. A wooden ramp led from the street level down into the yard. The exposed mooring stocks that lined the canals jutted blackly out of the moist, muddy ground. In the yard shipbuilders, oar makers, and lacquer painters were hard at work on vessels in various states of completion.

The elf addressed the nearest employee, who was shaving away at the unpainted form of a new vessel, whether there were any hearses ready to be picked up. He was referred to the person who handled customer relations at Bartolomeo's, a small brown-haired woman.

"This is the hearse your superiors ordered," she said. "It's been standing here for a while. We almost didn't think anyone would come and fetch it."

The hearse stood in a corner of the courtyard covered in a thick, paint-spattered wool blanket. When that was drawn aside the elf and the cat could take in the boat-hearse in all its funereal glory. It was shaped like the narrow craft that glided up and down the canals in the city, only set on a wooden undercarriage with large black wheels. In the front was a driver's seat. The elf leaned forward to look into the hull to assess whether there was enough space for the scientist's display, as well as two more people. The display had to be relatively lightweight, hanging from the church wall as it did, but the diameter of the outer cog wheels had looked considerable. About the length of a man? Something like that. If the largest wheels were stacked in the long direction on the hearse, they should fit exactly.

"This'll do," the elf said.

"Would you be needing a coffin as well?" The saleswoman motioned her hand toward a small stack of black and white coffins at the wall of the small enclosure. There were even a few smooth-surfaced headstones and some black tin lanterns as well.

The elf nodded. "Yes, one of the white coffins and two of the black lanterns, please."

"Will that be all?"

"Yes, that will be all," the elf said.

The woman smiled up at him with even white teeth and presented him with a beautifully tapered quill, an inkwell in cut glass, and an invoice for the clergy office for the cost of the new hearse. The elf signed it with a great flourish and a bow.

***

"You stole a hearse!" the cat said when they were out of the yard and back along the canals. "Do you really think Dame Logan and Alexandra will go with you to Spiral in a hearse?"

"Why on earth not?" asked the elf. "She's a scientist. She should not have any problems with hearses. And the coffin is just there to protect the display. You heard her say that they had to be very careful with the orbs."

The cat rolled her eyes. "She's an old woman! What do you think she'll say when she's asked to climb onboard a hearse?"

"She's not dead yet," the elf scoffed. "She's got nothing to fear. Besides, this way no one will stop us to examine what we are carrying. We'll go all the way to Spiral without as much as a hitch."

"Sometimes I want to bite you," said the cat.

They spent the night in a hovel by the docks. That was all the elf could pay for with his copper and tin coins. The room was tiny and smelled of hay, blood, and liquor. From the dingy tavern downstairs the sound of laughter, out-of-tune harmonica music, and sailor shanties was heard all night.

The bed was narrow and the mattress stuffed with straw, no eiderdown as in the hut by the beach. The cat refused to sleep in the moist, dirty bedding, claiming she would get lice in her coat. Thus, she lay on the elf's warm belly the entire night while the elf slept and dreamed of the mountains by the icy coast.

The next morning, the elf fed the cat fresh water and slices of ham by the public fountain in the square. He didn't dare go anywhere else in the city for fear of getting lost in the narrow streets and alleyways and canals and miss his appointment with the scientist. Therefore, he followed the exact same route to the ship builder as they had used the day before—errors and wrong directions and all.

At Bartolomeo's the hearse had been rolled up the back ramp to the sidewalk of the canal. The coffin and lanterns were placed in the bottom of the hull. The elf put his gray and black-maned horse in front of the wagon.

"I added a wide slow-burning candle to each of the lanterns as a gift from us," the saleswoman said.

"Thank you kindly," the elf replied and bowed at her.

The woman looked expectantly up at him.

"Yes?" the elf said, glancing down at her from the corner of his eye.

"Well, there is the matter of the first down payment ..." the woman said, a mildly embarrassed look on her delicate features.

In the corner of the shipyard, small and fenced in as it was, stood an aspen tree, modest and low, with boughs that rustled quietly in the wind. Its shivering foliage had already turned golden. In the next breath of wind that followed, the aspen leaves tinkled like coin and glittered of precious metal. The elf reached up and pulled off a handful of the aspen leaves and held them out in his narrow palm.

"Will this suffice as first payment," he asked and trickled the leaves down into her hands like the liquid assets she yearned for. As the leaves fell from the elf's white hands, they creaked and rustled like old paper, yet gleamed and glittered like gold.

The woman looked up at the elf, her eyes distant and cloudy as the autumn sky. "Oh yes, very much so. Thank you, good sir!" she said.

"HOW DID YOU do that?" the cat asked when they were standing at the canal, the black hearse gleaming next to them. "It was like magic, like sleight of hand!"

"Oh, that was easy," the elf replied. "Coin is merely the belief in the value attached to the objects serving as such. Simply an illusion."

The elf began to guide the horse and carriage along the canal.

"It's too heavy!" complained the cat. "There's no way I will be able to pull the hearse with the coffin and the display and you and the scientist and her grandchild in it! Never before in the long and glorious history of cats has anyone had the misfortune to be turned into a horse or having to live the humiliation of being put before a carriage. I won't do it! I just won't!"

"Not even if there were two of you?" the elf asked.

"Oh, no," said the cat and looked at him, the white showing in her dark horse eyes, her nostrils flaring. "Oh, no you don't!"

"Oh, yes," the elf laughed and duplicated the cat's horse body.

"What?" yelled the cat. Both dark grey horses made the same whinny of protest and whipped their long black tails in an identical, synchronous motion. "You copied me! I'm two! Oh, sweet dead cat gods, what have you done?"

"Relax," said the elf. "Just move your limbs as you always do and both your bodies will do the same. It's all you, anyway."

"Have you ever tried to do something and then you have two bodies doing the same?" the cat shouted in despair.

The elf considered. "Now that you mention it, not really."

"Turn me back at once!" yelled the cat.

"To one?"

"Yes!"

"But then you will have to pull the hearse all on your own."

At that the cat said nothing more but lowered her head. Large, glittering tears filled the green eyes of both horses, ran down their grey cheeks, and dripped into the canal below.

***

34

THE TWO HORSES that were the cat pulled the glistening black hearse slowly and mournfully to the church on the square. The elf sat on the driver's seat in his usual gray robes, but with the tall cylindrical hat of a hearse driver, flowing the end of a black scarf from it. The elf's hair was tied into a long tail at the base of his neck, and he was holding the reins loosely yet securely. The equipage looked almost like a proper funerary couch. As they walked up the last canal to the square a few of the noonday strollers stopped for the hearse and courteously inclined their heads as the black carriage passed them. The elf did his best to look somber but unaffected by the circumstances as he thought befitted his new and assumed station.

When the elf and the horses pulled up at the east door of the church they saw that the old scientist and her granddaughter had already taken down the planetary display. The brass gears and enameled orbs lay on a bed of yellow leaves according to diameter size and placement in the celestial sequence. It was a fascinating sight, as if the gears and cogwheels of the heavens had been dismantled.

Dame Logan was standing next to the display, where she was making certain that her granddaughter put the gears down on the leaves in the correct order. When she saw the hearse pulling up she turned and faced the elf.

"Master Elf, we will be ready for departure in about an hour. I take it you and the steeds are ready for the journey."

The elf bowed deeply to the old scientist. "Indeed we are, Dame Logan. I apologize for the somewhat unconventional style of carriage, but it was the only thing that was procurable within the bounds of this city."

At that the gray-haired woman started to laugh. She hadn't seen what kind of carriage it was before the elf pointed it out. He felt slight regret that he had mentioned it to the scientist. If he hadn't, maybe Logan wouldn't have noticed the unusual form of transport at all.

"I am, of course, not surprised, Master Elf," the old woman said. "I'm well aware of the state of horse-driven transport to and from the mainland. It's dismal, but we shall have to make the best of it. And I see you brought a coffin, too."

The elf reddened. "My apologies for the somewhat macabre choice, but since the hearse is open, I thought we might need something to store the more delicate parts of the display in."

Dame Logan's grin stretched her face into a hundred little wrinkles, and behind the half-moon shaped lenses of her spectacles, her eyes glittered. "Splendid thinking. Splendid thinking, young man!" cried the scientist. "What do we care about convention! We are scientists, theoretical and practical thinkers. Let the masses have their ideas about the macabre and the improper. We, on the other hand, shall have beauty and truth! Let's place the display into the casket at once!"

DAME LOGAN HAD had three large black bags made of the city's famous and frequently exported thick velvet. The bags were closed with broad black silk ribbons. The old woman ordered the elf to place the planets inside the small pouch, and the cogwheels and accompanying screws and brackets in the medium-sized bag. The remaining large bag contained the starry background, the thin base, and the crank that turned the entire display cog by cog.

Only the bag containing the planets was small enough to fit fully inside the coffin. The other bags were so large they prevented the lid from being closed, so that had to be left in the bottom of the vessel, leaning against the white-painted side of the coffin. But Dame Logan was nevertheless happy.

"Of course, my invention is greater than the sum of its parts," said the old scientist, "but some parts are more valuable than others. They were also the hardest to procure."

"They are made especially for the occasion?" asked the elf.

"The wheels are made after my exact specifications, but not the orbs themselves. Where do you think a scientist would have gotten the money to buy something like that?"

"Perhaps you are very rich?" suggested the elf.

That made Dame Logan laugh again. "Of course I'm rich, young man, but with knowledge, not coin. I invested all of my earnings from my lectures and treatises into constructing the brass wheels, the base, and the hood."

Does that mean she has no funds with which to pay for the journey, thought the elf before he remembered that his due for the journey was that which Dame Logan—and probably all other scientists—valued most of all—namely, knowledge.

"So where did the orbs come from?" pressed the elf. The moment the words left his mouth he regretted the question because suddenly he had a hunch he wasn't going to like the answer.

"From a royal collection of jewelry, gems, and toys," replied Dame Logan. "They were housed in the royal family's vault before I extracted them."

Behind the elf the horses whinnied loudly, sounding like laughter.

THE ELF LOOKED at the scientist. Apart from being an old woman and a scientist she was also a thief?

"And are these royals aware of your withdrawal from their vault?"

"They are now," replied Dame Logan. "That is not to say they like it, of course. In fact they decreed a high bounty on my head, the largest such a disgraceful boon has been announced in this part of the world."

"What?" said the elf. He was beginning to feel a little like the transformed cat.

"Come, come, don't look at me like that," Dame Logan said. "It's not like the king understood the scientific rationale behind the planetary models, and he certainly did not use them for anything productive. And I couldn't let those rare and extraordinarily accurate models be used as playthings for a three-year-old and then forgotten in a vault. I am no common thief."

No, just an extraordinary one, thought the elf, but wisely kept that to himself. Instead, he laughed nervously. "That is quite a story, Dame Logan," he said. "I do hope the matter has been resolved since that time and the decree graciously removed.

Now it was the old scientist's turn to look at him as if he were a fool. "Of course not!" Dame Logan said. "The decree still stands. Spiral's church even heightened the promised payment, as they deemed my scientific expositions unholy and subversive for the realm."

"But why do you wish to return to Spiral when you are outlawed there?" the elf asked.

"It is my birthplace," said Dame Logan, looking at the elf with an incredulous gaze. "My ancestors have lived there for generations. The academy where I was educated and to which I belonged for more than twenty years is there. I want my theorem to be included in Spiral's official description of the universe."

No less, thought the elf. "I do not see any way I can help you with that, Dame Logan," he said. "But I shall take you to Spiral as promised for a detailed lesson in the motion of the planets."

Logan nodded. "That is all I ask you to do. The rest is up to me."

("JUST ONE MORE question about this whole business, if you don't mind," asked the elf.

"Of course," Dame Logan said. "I quite enjoy talking about it. It was the adventure of my life, even though some may say that it wasn't right and that my dream of returning to the academy is an unrealistic one."

"Does the king of Spiral not know you are here?" the elf said. "I mean, if he wanted to make good on the bounty?"

Logan nodded. "Of course, their spies are keeping me under close surveillance. But the king cannot touch Canal as they are bound by an alliance and fortunately for me, an alliance of freedom and independence. Only if one of the two city states should be attacked by outside forces will they meddle in each other's affairs."

"But how is that enough to refrain Spiral from simply demanding to have you delivered to them on pain of breaking the alliance?"

"They would probably love to do that if it were within their powers," Dame Logan said. "But Spiral owes almost all its export and import to Canal. The only reason they are not already a subsidiary of Canal like the islands in the bay is that they are so far away from us and do not really offer much income for the merchants here, who earn much more by trading with the large states to the east and west. In addition, Canal is governed by merchants, not royals. They pay homage to the king of Spiral, but all they really concern themselves with is trade."

The elf nodded in reply but kept pondering the new information from the scientist. He couldn't help but feel a little twinge of sympathy for the old woman. She wanted to return to her home country and gain acceptance for her ideas there. But the old scientist's problems had little to do with the elf. He was not about to feel guilty for them.)

WHEN ALL THE parts of the planetary display had been loaded carefully and gently up into the coffin in the hearse the elf swung himself up in the driver's seat while the scientist and her granddaughter sat in the back. The hearse even had short transverse planks for sitting on just like vessels in Canal.

"Are you ready for departure to Spiral?" grinned the elf.

"Yeah!" Alexandra yelled and waved her arms. Even Dame Logan laughed. The horses whinnied and threw their manes and tails. Whether it was from excitement or annoyance it was hard to tell. The elf clicked his tongue and let the horses thunder across the cobbled square down the broad canal to the east and along the street toward the narrow causeway that barely bobbed its head above the ocean in the bay on its way to the mainland.

FOUR

IN THE FOREST OF FORGETTING

CANAL AND SPIRAL WERE SEPARATED BY a deep, dark forest. No one knew exactly how big it was or where it ended. The forest stretched out between the two cities like a shadow, and inside it, daylight rarely managed to reach the ground between the trees, even at midday in the summer. Canal and Spiral had once been one city under one form of government. But then the forest had started growing between the cities, expanding in itself, while turning more and more streets and buildings and stores and temples and parks and farms and villages into a part of the dark forest. Over the centuries the two cities grew farther and farther apart and developed in different ways. Canal became a city ruled by merchants and trade while Spiral was dominated by a dynasty of royals and mainly exporting knowledge—its scientists, ministers, and clergy traveling to all parts of the world. As the forest seemed to be still expanding, the two cities were still growing apart. Every year the forest bled more ground, more underbrush, more trees, and more forest to separate the two cities.

Most people feared the forest as it contained unfamiliar animals and plants and each year many people were lost in it. Even those who did not initially intend to enter the forest or pass through it on the way to the other city suddenly found themselves prompted to enter. And from there they continued deeper and deeper into the arboreal darkness until they vanished and were never seen again. Thus, the people of the divided city thought of the forest as a beast of its own, a living entity that needed sustenance, which it took from the hapless travelers that were lured deeper and deeper inside it. Perhaps they were the source of the forest's continued expansion?

THE HEARSE CROSSED the causeway at high tide. The ocean lapped at the water-smoothed stones that edged the narrow thoroughfare, yet did not reach the wheels of the peculiar looking hearse-boat; and the scientist, the girl, the elf, and the cat crossed safely to the mainland.

Along the wide bay many villages and farmsteads lay, vital contributors to Canal's wealth, trading with the city and providing its ample population with meat, grains, vegetables, fruits, and wines, as well as materials such as firewood, clay, ice, metals, and stone. In exchange for the constant, steady stream of consumables that were not available inside the city, Canal provided martial protection against the strange, scary creatures that sometimes burst out of the forest to attack and to the trade by the many sea routes that passed through Canal.

THE TWO GRAY horses kept a good pace along the narrow, winding path they followed into the forest. The path was completely barren of vegetation. Instead, it was bone white and made of sand packed so hard it was not possible to loosen anything from it. Even the horses barely left a mark on it. Yet, the path was only the width of a hand, so the hearse's wheels did not fit on it. Fortunately, the forest floor was covered with years of shed fir needles and except for the occasional mound of ferns, clumps of mushrooms, small stones, ant hills, or small stones, was flat and passable.

The two horses that pulled the hearse were still a cat and ran like cats do—fast and bounding and somewhat meandering through the landscape. The elf imagined the cat running in the knee-high grass at the cold coast in just that manner. Thus, the journey was not particularly smooth for the passengers, at least not in the beginning when the cat was still annoyed for having been duplicated and put before the hearse. The wheels banged against stones, or slid on moist pine needles, or noisily flattened slugs and toads that sat innocently on the forest floor while the cat ran on, ignoring the cart and its passengers. All the travelers could do was hang on with their hands on the edges and rails of the boat-hearse and ignore the bounces and skips as best they could.

The trees in the forest were dark firs with wide canopies and brown trunks that sat solidly in the ground. The broad skirts of the firs moved slowly in a wind the hearse's passengers did not notice, and the trees reached so far up into the darkness that it was not possible to see their arrowhead-shaped tops. The trees stood shoulder by shoulder, crowding each other in. Often it seemed that the hearse would not fit between the firs, but somehow, miraculously, the darkness between the scarred trunks widened, and the hearse passed beneath the guarding trees.

It was not possible to see far along the path. Only a few places the passengers could see the marrow-white trail snake ahead of them through the underbrush and a faint silvery light as if emitted from a hidden moon shone upon the trail. But for most of the journey the progression was hidden behind dark and secretive firs.

The passengers sat in silence. They were busy enough with trying to hang onto the cart as the cat bounded down the forest path. The elf had lit the lanterns and hung them at the front of the hearse so they lit the darkness in two small golden circles. The scientist and the girl had a small lantern of their own, which the girl clung tightly onto. Its tiny flame flickered and spat with every shake of the cart but remained miraculously burning.

Finally, the cat, tired and her frustration run out, meandered down the path by her own will, occasionally stopping to stroke her forehead against a protruding twig or sniffing on the smoking cap of a mushroom before continuing slowly on.

They followed the faintly moonlit path. Now that the creaking and banging from the tortured boat-hearse had silenced, they heard the sound of the forest itself. The wide firs made a low whooshing sound as they moved in the subtle wind. Occasionally, the staccato song or wooden clacking noises of birds broke the silence. Yet they never saw the creatures who were the source of these sounds. They also heard the soft sound of animal babies rolling on the leaves, of weevils eating through rotten wood, of small predators pulling even smaller prey by neck back to their underground hideaways. The more they listened to the forest the more sounds were revealed to them, a symphony of unseen and secret life flying and running and sneaking and plowing and leaping through the trees. They could also hear themselves more clearly than they ever had before—their heart beats, their breathing, their thoughts—and fell into a reverie of listening to their own sounds intermingle with the noises from the forest.

FINALLY, THE CAT stopped in a small clearing lit by the silver light from the unseen moon. There sat an almost completely obliterated ruin consisting of a few toppled columns and the crumbling remains of a wall covered with ferns, grass, yellow orchids, curling strands of ivy, and large bindweed flowers that shone in the pale light.

"This looks like as good a place to camp for the night as any," said the elf and jumped down from the driver's seat. The ground was strangely soft and giving but felt dry and whole. The elf stretched and rubbed his rump. He was a little sore after the cat's annoyed, wild rush through the forest.

Dame Logan also stretched and moaned as she got up. "The journey has not been kind to my back and hips," she complained.

"Wait, grandmother," Alexandra said. She quickly climbed over the side of the hearse, dropped down on the soft ground, and held out a supporting hand to her elderly relative. "Here, I'll help you down."

The old scientist took the hand and climbed slowly over the edge of the smooth, lacquered side.

"Time is not kind to the body. You will experience that someday yourselves, youngsters," Dame Logan said.

"Oh, grandmother," Alexandra sighed. "You always say that."

The elf smiled to himself but said nothing. Instead, he petted the horses and thanked them for their day's steadfast service. The horses whinnied a little sourly, and as soon as the elf let them out of the yoke, they immediately took to eating the tall grass at the outskirt of the clearing. They flicked their tails a few times like an annoyed cat but seemed quite pleased of the campsite nevertheless.

Behind the crumbling wall of the modest ruin, they discovered a human skeleton. It had been picked white by the forest's birds and furred hunters and insects and was half covered in curling fern stems and dark green moss that glittered with moisture. Any other signifier, such as clothes and jewelry and weapons, had been stolen, eaten, rusted, or buried.

The elf laid down on a patch of green moss on the other side of the low wall from the skeleton while the scientist and the girl went to rest in the bottom of the hearse. The horses curled up next to the toppled column, sniffed the green grass a little, and nibbled at it before they rested their heads on the ground and fell asleep with a loud simultaneous sigh.

The patch of moss and yellow orchids was a little moist from condensation, but the elf dried it quickly with a memory of a summer noon at the coast. A narrow ray of sunlight appeared at the patch, causing the yellow orchids to open fully and the moss to dry to a soft, thick living carpet. In the shaft of sun, small flesh-eating butterflies with orange wings and black markings danced. The elf put on his soft cloak with long hood and golden tassel hanging from its end and lay down on it. As soon as he stopped thinking about the sunlight, the bright shaft faded, giving way to the eerie silver light from beyond the tall treetops.

The wall fragment and the fallen column were so old and worn, their every indentation round and smooth. The stone itself was so eaten by wind and rain that it had begun to chip and flake in sheets like brittle sandstone. The elf moved his gaze across the pitted and pockmarked surface and slowly touched the decaying material. Tiny pebbles protruded from the soft stone, loose as rotten teeth. As the elf slid his finger across the surface, it crumbled a little more. Was this the visible mark of time passing? the elf wondered. Was time the process of nature disintegrating back into itself? If so, what would be the end of the journey and what would it look like?

When the elf fell asleep he dreamed that he was covered in leaves, then in snow, rushing water, and flower petals, alternating, fading, and returning as the seasons wore on. For an unknown length of time, he lay there until his meat melted off his bones and worms and weevils picked them clean, the soft velvet cloak nothing but a stripe of fabric next to him and his remains half hidden by grass that had grown fat and lush.

WHEN SOMEONE SHOOK the elf's shoulder and said his name he startled awake and prepared to shake leaves and petals from his clothes and hair. Instead, his dark cloak and gray robes were covered with sand and pebbles.

"Wake up," Dame Logan said. "You have been asleep for twelve hours already. It's time to get up and continue our journey."

"Hmm, what?" the elf said, still groggy from sleep. The smell of meat reached him. He sat up. "How do you know it's been twelve hours?"

"With this," Dame Logan said and put away the watch that was hanging from her pocket on a golden chain. "Here, have a sandwich and let's continue." The scientist handed the elf two thick slices of dark full-grained bread covered with grilled sunflower seeds moistened with cooking oil and having a few strips of smoked pork in the middle. The elf's stomach was growling for sustenance, so he ate it all before he drained some of the metal-tasting water in his canteen. He gave the rest to the horses, hoping they would find water farther into the forest.

The old scientist and the girl, even the cat, looked more subdued today than the previous evening.

"Is something the matter?" asked the elf. Even Alexandra sat on a log, hunched over with her elbows on her knees. Her hair had grown visibly, the disciplined edge of her straight bangs had lengthened and separated into impertinent tufts of dark hair.

"We'll never find our way out of the forest," Alexandra complained. "Let's go back."

"What do you mean, we'll never find our way?" the elf asked incredulously. "We're following a path that is as visible as moonlight on water."

"But we don't know where the path leads or when it'll end."

The elf scoffed. "It must end eventually somewhere close to Spiral. Besides, when your grandmother fled from that hoary old city, how did you get to Canal?"

"She went by ship, along the coast," Alexandra sighed. "The safe way."

***

ALEXANDRA AND DAME Logan packed their bags in silence and lifted them up into the hearse. But when the elf was putting the yoke back on the horses, the cat whinnied softly and hung her gray heads.

"Come now," the elf said. "I am not turning you back until we are out of this forest."

The horses nodded then, but their eyes remained half lidded and listless.

Sweet gods, is it just me who had a good night's sleep, the elf wanted to say. But he realized it might be rude and unnecessary to point it out and swung himself up in the driver's seat in silence. From there they continued along the bone-white path in the blue half-light.

The elf had worried the horses would bolt off after a good night's sleep and sustenance, but that fear turned out groundless. They started with a brisk pace, but it soon petered out into a slow, somber walk. The elf felt he had no thoughts in his head and no feelings in his chest and focused on keeping the horses on the lit path. The passengers were strangely quiet. Whenever they did speak it was in hushed and apprehensive tones. The elf didn't see what the others were so glum about but did nothing to break the unhappy silence.

They continued on for a very long time—the old scientist saying nothing, the girl saying nothing, and the elf so preoccupied with his own silence that he failed to notice that his passengers were growing more listless by the hour.

Finally, the path straightened a little so the elf and the horses could see farther down it. Now the strange blue light was directly ahead of them like an unblinking blue star. Yet no celestial body was visible between the trees. The boat-hearse pulled up at a broad clearing that was bathed by the blue light from the unseen moon. There sat an almost completely obliterated ruin consisting of a few toppled columns and the crumbling remains of a wall covered with ferns, grass, yellow orchids, curling strands of ivy, and large bindweed flowers that shone in the pale light.

***

NOT CARING FOR food or conversation, the elf dismounted and laid his cloak out on the ground by the column in the crumbling ruin. The old woman and the girl stood by the cart with their necks bent, seeming too tired to say or do anything.

Finally, Alexandra muttered, "This is the same clearing we spent the night in. We have been going in a circle the entire day."

"We have not!" scoffed the elf. He was tired and not in the mood for a discussion about geography and circumstance. "It's just a similar ruin. You told me yourself that areas of Canal and Spiral were taken over by the forest. Of course the ruins look similar. They originated in the same city." The elf pulled the cloak around him and rolled over on his side to sleep on the soft moss.

"Use your eyes, man!" yelled the girl. "Look, there's the ashes from our campfire. It even smells of the cooking oil I used! And there's the skeleton you unearthed." Alexandra pointed at a heap of bones that lay strewn in the grass at the periphery of the clearing. "Maybe the forest is trapping us here because you disturbed the remains?"

"Don't be ridiculous," countered the elf without looking at the girl and her grandmother. "Those are my remains, it is my grave, and I can disturb it all I want." Then he rolled over, closed his eyes, and fell asleep. On the fringes of sleep, he could hear Alexandra cry and the horses whinny sorrowfully.

THE PLAINTIVE NOISES seemed to go on all night. The elf wasn't sure how many hours of sleep he had, but finally he tired of the whining, threw his cloak aside, and stood.

Today there was no breakfast, no smoked meat, and no bread. No one said anything. Dame Logan now looked visibly older, and her granddaughter had become a mature woman.

They both looked hollowed-eyed and sat hunched over. Even Alexandra looked wizened—like she had skipped youth and adulthood and gone directly to old age. They climbed into the hearse with slow, reluctant movements.

When the elf climbed up into the driver's seat the horses gave a loud sigh and lowered their eyes before they slowly began to walk. Annoyed and still sleepy, the elf clicked his tongue, shook the reins, and shouted at the horses to have them move faster.

"What's the point?" croaked Dame Logan. "We'll just end up at the same spot tonight, anyway. We're driving in circles."

"Absolutely not," protested the elf. "We'll get there when we get there. Have some faith!"

It was a long day. Or night. It was hard to say in the dark forest under the dark sky in the strange blue light. Fortunately, the complaints from the old woman and the girl quieted down after a little while. But it gave way to something worse. A brooding, depressed silence. Both the scientist and her apprentice looked weighted down with a great sadness and sat motionless in the hearse. Every time the elf turned around to see if they were still there the two of them just sat there staring into the bottom of the hull not saying a word.

The old scientist's hair had grown longer and whiter. The girl had visibly hunched. The horses walked with bent necks and heavy heads, their feline pride gone, even the eagerness to return to their original form. Thus, the hearse moved more and more slowly. The elf had long since fallen into a timeless reverie where he thought about nothing and felt nothing, just stared at the path and the blue light beyond it. When he noticed they had stopped altogether he had no idea how long they had been standing still.

The horses had laid down in the middle of the path. The elf rose to climb down from the hearse. In front of him was a small clearing lit by the blue light from the unseen moon. There sat an almost completely obliterated ruin consisting of a few toppled columns and the crumbling remains of a wall covered with ferns, grass, yellow orchids, curling strands of ivy, and large bindweed flowers that shone in the pale light.

THE ELF WASN'T surprised. He had in his heart of hearts known they would end up there. He just didn't want to admit it to himself or his passengers. He bowed his head in silent defeat, smoothed down his long black hair a few times, then crouched down by the two gray horses.

"How are you feeling, old friend?" the elf asked the cat. The horses were on their sides in the wet grass. Now they turned their heads slightly and blinked up at the elf as if they just now discovered that he was there. The elf reached forward and petted the gray heads on their soft muzzle. The horses made a strange grunting sound and pushed at his hand. He realized the cat was trying to purr.

"Please don't let me die a horse," the cat begged. "Turn me back."

The elf shook his head slowly. "You're not going to die. At least not now."

"Yes, I am," said the cat. "The forest won't let us leave—just like it lets no one go through it."

Tears stood in the elf's eyes. Had he saved the cat from starvation at the coast only to let her lose faith inside the endless forest? "We are almost there," the elf said.

"How can we be?" asked the cat. "We have been going in circles for three days and found nothing but forest. We don't even have water."

"The city is just around the corner," the elf said. "It's right across the clearing behind those trees. I know it." He closed his eyes. He could hear the sound of seagulls floating on a coastal breeze above vessels that bobbed up and down on the gray water in the harbor. Behind the narrow masts and flying sails, gray clouds flew past in the windy, overcast sky. The elf could almost hear the sound of the waves lapping against the old granite quay and the noise of the boats shifting in their anchorage. On the wind the scent of lemons, leathers, and incense drifted on the wind from the market.

"Yes, I can hear it and smell it," said the horses that were really a cat. On the other side of the clearing, a faint light shone through the dark branches of the firs. The elf looked more closely. He had never been to Spiral, but through the wall of trees, he thought he could see white seabirds hovering on a cool breeze. Above him the city spread out on a wide plain that spiraled upward in the sky ever higher like the shell of some of the soft-fleshed creatures that undulate over the seabed at night.

The City of Spiral looked like a gigantic conch buried vertically in the ground, the walls of its shell having been worn away over the eons by rain and wind but the flat parts of the structure higher and higher to impossible heights. From the ground it looked like the spire at the very top of the spiral touched the gray clouds themselves, and from it shone a light as bright as the sun. Occasionally, hapless travelers or despairing nobles threw themselves off the rail-less edge of winding levels to fall crashing down on the white mother-of-pearl on the plateau below. More common and even less sanitary was the habit some noble and royal housemaids had of pitching the stinking contents of chamber pots and spittoons down onto the rooftops and gardens below.

BUT IT WAS no wonder. As the geography and the architecture of Spiral itself was rigidly stratified, so was social and personal life. Everyone in the royal stratum had to be born of the royal family. That meant a life in luxury literally high above the stations and circumstances of the nobles, the clergy, scholars, and merchants below. However, it did not necessarily mean a good position in the royal world. Were your father and mother not of a high enough station or held enough money, you were appointed the glorious service of royal chamber maid, cook, stable hand, manservant or other servile capacity. There just wasn't room enough for a hundred different kings and queens and princes and princesses at the top. Even there, someone must be lower, do the dirty work, and serve the others of their station.

And as above, so below. All the lower strata were organized similarly. The servants and guards and craftsmen of any level were from the same stratum, but those of a higher level were richer and lived in better conditions than those on the shelf below. This was The Brilliance, the Glorious City of Spiral. Now it shone through and above the trees of the impenetrable forest and the eerie blue light.

"COME!" YELLED THE elf and immediately turned the horses back to their feline shape before picking the cat up and placing her on his shoulder. The cat, so happy to be back to her original form, celebrated by promptly falling asleep. The elf cradled the cat in his sash and tied it around her so he could carry her like an infant. Then the elf ran over to the hearse and took the largest and heaviest of the velvet bags. "Dame Logan, Dame Logan!" the elf shouted. "Look! Spiral is close! Let us depart while we can!"

The old scientist glanced up, hollow cheeked and ashen grey. "Please don't disturb a dying woman, Master Elf," she said. "Even if you yourself are hale and happy. It's rather rude, you see." But then Dame Logan lifted her heavy head and saw the twisting form of Spiral peek over the dark firs. She jumped up, brushed off her dark robes, and took the smallest velvet bag from the hearse.

"Stop bothering me," Alexandra moaned when the elf toed her on the shoulder. Her face and hands were lined, and her back bent like an old person.

"Look, my granddaughter!" the old scientist yelled, her dying obviously forgotten. She stabbed her index finger into the sky. "Look! Spiral! We made it!" Dame Logan and the elf hauled Alexandra on her feet and threw the remaining velvet bag in her lap.

All three of them ran across the clearing past the old ruin and dove into the trees and bushes that separated the forest from the city. They tumbled out of the vegetation and onto the ancient mother-of-pearl docks that constituted the lowest section of the bottom tier of the city. Above them the sky was gray and windy, and the air carried the scent of lemons, leathers, and incense from the market just up from the docks.

WHITE AND GRAY and yellow and red and brown sails flapped in the wind. The vessels they belonged to were of all shapes and sizes—from galleys that came from the other side of the ocean to barques, brigs, and schooners from much farther down the coast to rowboats from the isles in the bay. Some were sleek and elongated with hundreds of oars bristling from two levels in their sides. Others sat high in the water, had masts like small forests and captain's quarters with windows in gleaming glass. Other ships were open with a single deck, a large sail, and winged worms curling along the stern and aft.

On the thoroughfare, pedestrians, riders, carriages, and coaches passed them. The air was thick with footfalls and voices, calls and cries. At the end of the docks, containers, crates, chests, boxes, and barrels of all kinds stood waiting to be carried onboard the vessels to the far reaches of the world or were on their way farther up into the city and the markets in the higher strata. No item and no shipment passed through to the upper levels without having passed customs on the docks. Here a third of the item's value was deducted in tribute to the nobles, who again passed a third of what they earned upward to the royal family.

The scientist and the girl and the elf dusted sand and moss from their clothes and followed the white planes above them up into the sky all the way to the white spire far above them that seemed to pierce the clouds themselves. They had arrived in the city of Spiral.

FIVE
LADY KNIGHT AND THE SUN

THE ELF INSTINCTIVELY HATED THE PLACE. He hated the pristine white mother-of-pearl, how it spiraled haughtily into the heavens and the way it created a strictly compartmentalized vertical hierarchy. Because as the white spiral grew narrower and narrower toward the top, it could accommodate fewer and fewer people. There was not room for everyone at the top. The elf remembered the spaciousness, the openness, and the silence of his origins at the cold coast and inwardly rebelled against the hierarchy the white city imposed on its populace by way of its form alone. The elf nevertheless did not voice the opinions that burned in his chest like embers. Instead, he turned calmly toward the scientist. "Please let me have a moment to procure something for the cat," the elf said. He turned and walked over to a merchant's booth nearby and paid two of his copper coins for a small packet of dried fish. That was a peace offering for the cat when she woke up. She was still asleep inside the elf's sash.

"What's next?" the elf asked when he returned to the scientist and the girl.

"We go see some of my old colleagues," Dame Logan said.

Dame Logan strode along the wide curve of the docks and up onto the main thoroughfare of the city that curled all the way to the lofty upper reaches of the kingdom. The bottom spiral was the widest and the most populous. It was filled with small shops, smithies, tanneries, workshops, guest houses, and private homes—even tiny chicken, rabbit, and pigeon coops crammed against one another shoulder to shoulder. The lower circle looked like any large city in the region—dirty, smelly, and noisy, with mud slicking the cobbles and rain graying the half-timbered buildings. The fact that over half the city sat high above the ground did not stop the population from going about the business of an ordinary town. Occasionally, carriages of glistening lacquer, resembling that of the vessels in Canal, but in bold colors. One was red, another dark green, one dark purple, and another had the hue of recently made rich cream.

"Whose carriages are those, grandmother?" Alexandra asked.

"Those are the colors of the scholars, the guardians, the nobles, and the royals," Dame Logan said. The elf, scowling, made note of the transportation of the higher-ups.

AS THEY CONTINUED up the main thoroughfare, something quick and slinky grazed their legs, tittered, and ran off.

"Eww, was that a rat?" Alexandra commented inside the din of the crowd.

"Yaouw!" the cat shouted and jumped down from the elf's shoulder and down on the sandy mother-of-pearl.

"Hang on!" the elf gasped, but the cat was already lost between the moving forest of feet and legs that surrounded them.

"Now what?" Dame Logan said, irritated. She was trying to glance over the heads of the crowd as they were moving along with it so they didn't accidentally flow with the mass of people to the edge of the tier and fall off.

"No!" the elf yelled after the cat. "Come back!"

"Wait!" Dame Logan shouted and managed to grab hold of the elf's sash just before he dove into the crowd, hunched and running almost on all fours, to be able to see the cat between the legs.

"Nyar!" the cat yowled, unable to contain herself in excitement and hunting fervor. That rude rodent who had run past her like she was a harmless rabbit or worse, a dog, was going to get it! Soon it would feel the force of her death bite as it closed over its neck. She clattered her teeth eagerly and continued to bound after the scent of the dirty beast.

"Where are you all going?" Alexandra cried behind them.

THE CAT DUCKED and wove between the legs and turned a corner so fast it was for a moment like she was running on the same spot without getting anywhere until her small but sharp claws found purchase on the smooth mother-of-pearl, whose thin cover of gravel and sand she kicked up like a speeding horse.

"No!" the elf yelled, suddenly fearful that the cat would vanish forever, and pushed his way through the crowd. But since the rat and the cat were running in the opposite direction of the endless flow of people, it took him considerably longer to negotiate the crowd than the cat. As a result, Dame Logan and Alexandra had no problems spotting him and keeping up.

The cat darted here and there following the track of the obnoxious rodent that weaved in between the legs and feet. The cat, an experienced mouser from the meadows around the hut at the coast in the north, and making up for the rat's head start with pure determination and will, slowly gained on the fleeing rat. When the rat saw this in the corner of its eye it quickly veered to the right until it almost hit a wall so worn the wood was fuzzy with splinters and slipped in between a crack in the half-timbered surface. The cat immediately saw that she was too large to fit into the crack and let out a blood-curdling yowl. She continued along the wall until she found a narrow door and bounded inside, her rear legs and tail the last the elf spotted.

"In here, quick," the elf waved at Alexandra and ducked inside the creaking doorway before she could follow.

"Over here, grandmother!" Alexandra yelled, jumping up and down until she saw that Dame Logan had spotted her over the heads of the moving crowd. She then followed the elf into the darkness.

"Oh, for heaven's sake!" Dame Logan huffed, collected the hem of her robe, and pushed her way through the throng after them.

THEY FOLLOWED THE elf into the dark corridor. It was so narrow they bumped into the walls at both sides and creaked so loudly they had no problems confirming the presence of one another in the darkness.

"Here, kitty! Here, here!" the elf kept squawking as he followed the path he somehow sensed that the cat had taken. But a little while into the darkness, his shins hit something hard, bringing his progress to a painful halt. He pitched forward into the darkness, throwing his hands up in front of him. The palms of his hands slammed into a wooden plank in the horizontal and then one more, a little farther up. A staircase! The elf scrambled up the uneven, slanting stairs while the ancient wood creaked and popped.

"There's a staircase farther inside. Watch out, grandmother!" Alexandra yelled. She could hear the swishing and swushing of Dame Logan's many layers of starched and stiffened scholar robes behind her.

"Dear gods," the scientist sighed, out of breath and hair bun askew.

The elf raced up the narrow staircase, hands on the next steep, uneven step to prevent from falling. Now his eyes had adjusted to the darkness, and he could make out a faint outline of a doorway farther up. He kept climbing while he shouted for the cat, which was of course nowhere to be seen in the darkness.

Finally, he was up. The elf half jumped, half fell headlong out of the doorway and out on a wooden floor as uneven and creaking as the staircase. Here a series of wooden Y-shaped pillars fanned out in a semi-circle, supporting a mezzanine that followed the length of the circular room. From the pillars hung lit oil lamps that were burning with the low, soot-filled flame of mixed animal fats. But the elf had no time to take in his surroundings beyond scanning frantically for the cat and yelling for her.

Only a fool would think any animal—domestic or wild—would seek out the source of such noise—especially not a cat, who would prefer a quiet, relaxed atmosphere to loud noises and talk. But the more the elf shouted for the cat and the longer she stayed away, the more the elf had the feeling of being ignored.

"Kitty! Kitty, where are you?" he shouted and ran beneath the mezzanine to scan for the cat in the dark shades from the flickering lamps. Finally, in the dark corner where the balcony ended in a blank wall, the elf stopped, not seeing the cat anywhere, and was overcome with grief. The cat would never return. He would never see her again.

When he had managed to convince Dame Logan to make him her apprentice and finished his apprenticeship he would have to return to the coast in the north on his own. There he would enter the small and lonely hut on the beach, close the door quietly behind him, and lay down on the narrow bed covered in eiderdown and straw all alone. He had lost his furry friend, and now he would never see her again. It felt like a piece of himself had vanished. He buried his face in his hands and cried, quietly at first, but then louder and louder as he started heaving for air.

"CAREFUL, GRANDMOTHER," ALEXANDRA said and helped her grandmother up the last step. On the other side of the room, she saw the elf crying. On the stage to her right, a small group of people were staring at the elf. They wore no arms or uniforms, but simple, drab clothing like the throng of townspeople that passed by outside. They seemed to have just become aware of the elf's presence, so Alexandra decided to try to get him out before anyone else reached him.

"Come on," Alexandra said, tugging at the elf's sleeve.

"No, we can't leave without the cat," the elf said, pulling his arm out of her grip.

"The cat will find us when she's killed whatever it was she ran after," Alexandra said, and took the elf's arm again. The elf was tall, but so was Alexandra; and she started dragging him by his long, tapering sleeves.

The elf sniffled and followed her a few steps, but then stopped. "No, no," he whimpered. "I have to wait for her. What if she doesn't come back?"

He broke into tears again.

Alexandra rolled her eyes. "You haven't lost your teddy! Besides, with all that crying, the cat will hear you fine. She'll come when she's finished with whatever cat-things she's doing. Come now."

"No," the elf wept. "She's never been here before. She'll get lost, and I'll never see her again."

"Come on now, hurry!" Dame Logan said, motioning at them from the doorway. Even the short, tight movement of her limbs showed that she was quickly losing her patience.

"You, there!" a voice yelled from the stage.

"Oh, no," Alexandra said. She slipped behind the elf and started pushing him in the direction of the door.

"No, please wait!" A small man jumped down the modest height from the stage to the straw-covered floor. He was neither young nor old, but balding and had pulled the tufts of sandy-colored hair that remained over to one side. His long vest and jacket, knee-long breeches, and polished boots so different from the long pantaloon and short jackets worn by the common townsfolk told Alexandra he was some sort of boss.

"No worries," Alexandra said. "We're already leaving."

"Are you the traveling actors we're expecting?" the man said.

"No," Alexandra said. Did they really look like that? It must be the elf who gave that impression with his long sleeves and even longer hair. She and Dame Logan wore scholarly robes befitting their places in the hierarchy as master and apprentice.

Across the room Dame Logan crossed her arms over her chest. Alexandra nodded in reply. Her grandmother was getting seriously annoyed.

"What do you need actors for?" the elf sniffled. Maybe if he could continue the conversation and thus delay his forced departure, he would be able to spot where the cat went.

"Two of them have eloped with one another, and the replacements have fallen ill," the little man said. "We have sent message for other actors. We need them for the premiere tonight."

"Of what play?" the elf asked, as if he were familiar with any of them, and twisted like a fish out of Alexandra's grip.

"*Lady Knight and the Sun*," the man said as though it were a given. "I'm Valentinelli, the director and conductor of this play, and you'd be perfect for it," he said and turned to Alexandra.

THE PLAY WAS an operatic version of the famous fable of Lady Knight. It required a young woman tall and broad-shouldered enough to carry the ornate, expansive theatrical armor that symbolized the noble knight and to give a believable impression of martial prowess and stamina enough to slay dragons. In addition, Director Valentinelli explained, the person playing the lady must exhibit the grace of a young woman of good background and the confidence and eloquence of a well-educated mind. Since the acting was separated from the singing (because it was almost impossible to find someone with the right stature and voice), it entailed mostly mock combat and moving back and forth across the stage at the right time.

Alexandra, who had always had a secret liking for stage plays and an even more secret desire to act in one, frowned but stopped pushing the elf and let the Director explain the play and their duties to them.

Dame Logan initially intended to veto the idea, but then she saw the short breeches and long coat of a minor nobleman, albeit in the drab colors and coarse fabric of one of the noble servant families that lived to serve their more prestigious and powerful peers. Dame Logan immediately entered the negotiations with the verve and vigor of an old manager and managed to get Valentinelli to promise them not only a pass to the next tier in the city but also a payment in coins large enough to bribe guardians at the gate should the pass somehow fail to elicit the desired effect.

Thus, all three felt they gained something of the deal: Dame Logan, the access to the next level she wanted; Alexandra, a shot at the stage; and the elf, a prolonged stay in the building that he was certain the cat was rummaging around in. He hoped with a yearning that startled him a little in its strength that she would reappear in.

LADY KNIGHT WAS the Champion of Spiral of old. The present-day monarch had descended directly from her. She faced and defeated its enemies while her mother, Queen Moon, organized its people in response to crises. After three years of summers so rainy and sunless only the fishermen, crayfish catchers, mussel gatherers, and the seaweed harvesters in the bay around Spiral had any sustenance to deliver to the city, Lady Knight was sent out to find the sun. She searched all corners of the land from high to low and east to west. Finally, some migrating sparrows told her they had last seen the moon above the dark forest that surrounded Spiral. Lady Knight spurred her old stud and rode to the dark forest as quickly as her steed could run. There she entered a sunless, arboreal world where only the moon lit the path pale and thin like bone. Deep inside the forest, Lady Knight found the sun captured and hung up inside a glass lamp by none other than the Faerie King and his court. The forest was so dark not even the sun's lamp could illuminate it but shone pale and blue through the glass of the lamp like a second moon.

"Release the sun immediately," Lady Knight demanded, pulling the reins of her horse so he reared up in the most fearsome manner. "The sun's light and warmth belong to everyone, not just you," Lady Knight declared, pointing her sword at them.

The fair folk hissed and drew away from her and the gleaming silver of her weapon, which no fair folk like, until the Faerie King himself appeared, tall and with hair like a black waterfall. He challenged Lady Knight to a duel, but she refused, saying she was no common gladiator. The Faerie King's trickery was famous throughout the land.

Instead, the Faerie King bade her do three deeds of heroism for him. If she survived, she'd have the sun. If not, she'd have to be the Faerie King's bride for all eternity.

Thus, Lady Knight went off to slay the seaworm of the north, the troll in the east, and the swan of the south. But the Lady didn't smite these giants as the Faerie King had told her to because they were his enemies. Instead, she asked them of the Faerie King's weakness in promise of sparing them. This was not an entirely peaceful affair, but after losing a tail, an eye, and a leg to the Lady Knight, each giant relented and promised to reveal the Faerie King's weakness.

Then she traveled back to the dark forest with the tail of the sea serpent, the eye of the troll, and the leg of the swan, and announced it to the Faerie King.

"Splendid," the Faerie King said. In secrecy he drew his foil of moonbeams and gnarled branches and prepared to run it through the Lady Knight as she knelt to offer her sacrifices. Instead, the Lady Knight flicked the poison of the sea serpent so the Faerie King was blinded for a moment. Then she held the petrifying eye of the troll up to stop the Faerie King in his tracks before she whipped the gut-rending claw of the swan of the south toward the Faerie King's concave waist.

"No, don't!" the Faerie King shouted before Lady Knight could cleave him in two.

"Then release the sun," Lady Knight demanded.

The Faerie King had to do it himself. Lady Knight would not even let one of his courtiers do it for him. She took the string that the sun was attached to and cut off a small piece of it. With this she bound the Faerie King and let him sit in the clearing of his forest while she rode away with the sun now captured. The Faerie King howled with humiliation, but none of his underlings could free him. With much reluctance and many tears, the Faerie King chose to sacrifice his left hand to free himself from the string that had held the sun.

With the sun to light her path, the Lady Knight found her way out of the dark forest. "There," the sun said. "Now release me and I will return to my rightful place in heaven."

The Lady Knight didn't reply. She checked that the sun's bonds were well fastened to her saddle and brought it to her home at the top of Spiral. There the sun was bound to the spire of the giant shell so it never could be captured by anyone else and vanish again.

To this day the Faerie King still weeps inside his lightless forest, and the sun, forever bound to Spiral's enormous nacre, dims every night to mourn her lost freedom.

***

"Now I understand why the words in the lyrics of this operatic play are happy but sung on a sad note," Alexandra said when they had been given their lines and shown where to stand and walk and exit in the play.

"It's rubbish," Dame Logan growled. She had been roped in to play the Mother Queen, but all she had to do was stand in the background with the choir for most of the time. "This is just a stupid fairytale! It doesn't say anything correct about the sun at all."

"But isn't this what most people in Spiral believe in?" Alexandra asked.

"Yes, unfortunately," Dame Logan sighed.

"Even the scholars and researchers?"

"Not the part about Faerie Kings and monstrous giants, of course," Dame Logan said, much more quietly, making sure most of the other actors were out of earshot. "But scientific theories as to why the sun circles the Earth."

"But are they any sound?" Alexandra said, which she had been trained to always ask, especially when it came to scientific theories as well as popular beliefs, and which she did with the sharp impatience and desire for change typical of the young.

"At least sound enough not to easily accept other theories," Dame Logan said.

Their duties as actors were simple. When the Conductor-Director waved small triangular flags whose colors corresponded to their roles they should move across the stage from left to right in rhythm with the music. There singers in all black at the back of the stage would perform the arias while the actors emoted the events described in the songs. This pantomime was highly stylized in set patterns that repeated themselves throughout the play. The biggest challenge was to learn the basic combination of movements and positions required for the role. These were repeated and reused throughout the play. Most of the morning went to having the enormous, brightly colored costumes fitted because there would be no time to change into them before the premiere that night. They were large and expansive but made of lightweight materials such as summer silk and taffeta and balsa wood for the standing collars, basket-like underskirts, and mock weapons. They got into the costumes, their faces whitened into masks, then painted to the unrecognizable. The final touch was enormous wigs of dyed wool and stiff marsh cotton, equally expansive hats, and glittering stage jewelry made from prisms of colored glass.

In full costume they looked three times their normal size, and it was easy to understand why the actors' movements were slow and ritualized instead of quick and realistic. There was so much to carry. Alexandra, Dame Logan, and the elf looked at each other and laughed, widened and heightened as they were from their tall, broad costumes. They almost forgot the vanished cat.

They had a small break where all they had was dark lukewarm ale and nothing else to eat, which made them lightheaded, but which nevertheless sated them and quenched the thirst they had worked up carrying the exaggerated costumes around the stage. The rest of the afternoon went to learning the sequence of songs in the play and what flags and cues to look for to enter the stage and perform another round of highly patterned and stylized acting.

During the rehearsal it became clearer to them that they were simply lending their bodies out to the costumes themselves, which remained the same no matter who played the roles. They were simply vehicles for the story itself and were less there to project any realistic personality traits or peculiarities of the individual roles themselves. Thus, it became easier to shed self-consciousness and feelings of being awkward and follow the rise and fall and motion of the music.

***

FINALLY, VALENTINELLI SHOUTED, "That's great! Now, let's do it one more time from start to finish. This time with an audience present."

And now when they gazed out into the darkness past the stage kit by flickering thick oil and smoky torches, the small circular space was packed with people who were sitting or lounging or standing in the back.

They were chatting and eating and drinking while vendors selling dark ale and even darker bread offered their wares to the public. Many seemed to have brought food and drink with them. A few seemed to have brought straw baskets but pulled nothing out of them. The new actors were quickly informed that those bags contained heads of old cabbage, potato, and fish to be thrown at everyone on the stage and in the orchestra pit if the performance was deemed unsatisfactory.

The newly minted actors swallowed a bit nervously and faltered a little in their slow, measured steps across the dirty wooden stage, but the song and music and the ritualistic nature of the motion slowly took them away again until there was only the song, the music, and the stage.

The audience cheered with the Lady and booed at the Faerie King and laughed when the giants were mock-slain, their actors unfurling lengths of red ribbon in lieu of blood and falling to the floor emoting wildly. The atmosphere seemed fairly good. No one had forgotten that often where to stand or where to go at what moment. When they did, the music covered for the slight hesitation or imperfect positioning on the stage. No smelly leaves of cabbage or gaping heads of fish had been pelted on the stage, nor had any of those in the audience who were not yet drunk fallen asleep.

But then, as the play was drawing to a close and the Lady Knight was emoting during the last aria, the Faerie King lying curled up on the floor cradling the hand he had had to sacrifice for his freedom, a long, lonely wail was heard from the side of the stage. It took a few yowls before anyone really noticed the caterwauling, and by then, a small, somewhat bewildered gray creature dared to come out on the stage, where she stood peering over at the bled-out Faerie King on the floor. The cat—because it was none other than her—was finally done chasing the rude rat in the walls. She had no problems recognizing the elf inside the large overdone costume. But there were so many large stomping feet in the way, and why wasn't her master sitting up and giving her attention after he had made such a ruckus earlier when she ran?

Skittish but determined, the cat ran out onto the stage while she jumped and startled from the movement of the legs and feet around her. By now the entire audience had spotted her and was laughing and pointing and cheering her on. It was like watching a small animal trying to cross a busy road. When there was a tiny gap in the movement of feet and rustling of long robes the cat threw herself forward and rushed toward her goal.

When she finally reached the elf he immediately sat up and yelled, "Kitty!" He pushed the painted papier mache helmet and giant wig off his head. Director Valentinelli saw everything but decided to go with it and kept conducting. The chorus was singing, and Alexandra finished raising her arms to heaven to place the sun at the tip of Spiral's spire while the cat climbed the elf's shoulders and enthusiastically licked his face and hands like a small but very loving dog to the applause and laughter of the audience.

"Too bad they didn't use the old version of the play," Dame Logan said backstage, pulling off her tall, spiral-shaped red wig when they were finished bowing and reentering the stage for more bows and the audience had begun to leave the premises.

"The old version?" Alexandra said. "How did that go?"

"There the Lady Knight and the Faerie Elf were one and the same—only two sides of the regent's mind who fought over the right and wrong self-conduct and the captive of our basic awareness, or consciousness, that is always present—like the sun behind the clouds," Dame Logan said.

"Really?" the elf said. "That sounds intriguing. Why was a new version made?"

"Isn't that obvious?" Dame Logan replied, looking at him like he was the dumbest creature on the planet. "It was too difficult to understand and had to be simplified so everyone could get what the story was about."

SIX

THE ACADEMY OF NATURAL SCIENCES

ALEXANDRA, DAME LOGAN, THE ELF, AND the cat continued uphill along the wide slant of mother-of-pearl, carrying the black velvet bags with the precious models of the planets slung over their shoulders. The crowd that filled the road seemed to be in constant motion, surging toward the tier's upper gate. The people were carrying bags, rucksacks, barrels, crates, or chests of all possible and seemingly impossible shapes and sizes.

"NOW WE REALLY could have used the hearse we left behind at the docks," Alexandra shouted over the din of the throng.

The elf covered the cat's ears with his palms. "Don't remind her of having been transformed into two horses!" he yelled. "Or she might run off again."

"But why aren't we taking a carriage, grandmother?" Alexandra insisted.

"Because we will need to disembark and hail a new carriage once we get to the stratum gate!" cried the scientist without turning. She then had to throw up her arms to shield herself from the angrily beating wings of a white swan and the frantic flapping of a male peacock that were carried by their feet on a long stick over someone's shoulder.

"Why can't the carriage go from here all the way to where we're supposed to be?" Alexandra yelled.

"Don't be uncouth, dear," Dame Logan shouted in reply. "Or stupid!"

"Because the tiers above the station you belong to are all closed to you, but not for someone from higher up," the elf said. He had started to realize how things worked in Spiral.

"Oh," Alexandra said. "That's really silly."

The elf laughed at the immediacy and honesty of Alexandra's conclusion.

"But can't we just switch carriages when we get to the gate?"

"We're not going farther than the next stratum, anyway," Dame Logan said. "It's not far."

That turned out to be incorrect. The width of Spiral's lowest stratum of flat nacre was enormous, easily the size of several fields. They walked and walked while the black velvet bags grew heavier and heavier on their backs and the crowd seemed to grow denser and denser until they had to forcibly push their way ahead. But finally the mother-of-pearl narrowed to a passage the width of a road before it ended at a natural constriction, the transition from one chamber in the gigantic shell to the next. This constriction's nacre had been carved into wreaths of roses, ivy, and lily of the valley.

Six guardians with red armor and red spears blocked the gate. Here the crowd delivered their goods, placed the crates, caskets, barrels, satchels, sacks, and chests they were carrying in stacks on the dirty mother-of-pearl. Cows, sheep, goats, pigs, deer, moose, chickens, ducks, turkeys, pheasants, ptarmigans, quails, and pigeons stood in tiny cages, mooing and braying and hissing and clucking and quacking. Reed baskets containing fruits or vegetables, fish, crabs, lobsters, round bread, long bread, flat bread, bird eggs, fish roe, sacks of fine or whole-grained flour, bolts of fabrics in all colors, huge balls of dyed and uncolored yarn, hammers, tongs, spades and other metal tools, an armory's worth of spears, halberds, sabers, rapiers, daggers, arquebuses, crossbows, even a cannon stood by the gate. Fresh clay, wood, furs, leathers, dyes, inks, paper, and every other raw or lightly processed material imaginable was present, too. All of it was heaved through the gate, shifted by a chain of human beings, and slung from hand to hand to the other side. There other hands lifted the variegated burdens up on their backs for continued transport farther up into the city. But none of the workers passed through the gate themselves.

"Legend has it that if a person from the lowest stratum reaches the uppermost plateau, the whole city will crumble," Dame Logan yelled. The comment garnered a few glances from the closest workers, but the old scientist didn't notice. "That is, however, only one of the reasons why no one from the lower stages are allowed through the gate. Should anyone force their way in, they will be hurled off the edge of Spiral."

Nice, thought the elf, but said nothing. How on Earth did the old scientist plan to get them through the gate? But he hadn't to worry. The issue was apparently also on the old woman's mind. She pushed her way to the elf and prodded him in the side.

"When we come to the arch," Dame Logan whisper-shouted into the elf's ear. "Look at me and just follow. Think of the planetary display, think of what you have learned from it and what questions you have about it, and make that rise to your body and face. Think scholarly thoughts and let them show!"

***

As they came closer to the gate, they saw that it was blocked with goods and people sending them through to the other side. The old scientist straightened her back, lengthened her stride, and headed for the gate without looking at the soldiers and their spears that gleamed even in the light of the overcast day. The elf did as he had been asked and copied the old woman's walk. So did Alexandra. She immediately looked older than before.

"Halt!" one of the guards shouted and stepped out to bar Dame Logan's progress.

"Who dares interrupt the progress of the Master Scholar of the Fifth Tier of the Academy of Natural Sciences?" Dame Logan shouted.

Upon hearing this, the guard bowed deeply, and said, "Forgive me, Master Scholar, but I need to know who your companions are."

The old scientist huffed loudly. "What nerve! The Head of the Academy will be hearing about this. But if you must ask," Dame Logan said and motioned at the elf, "this is a scholarly master like myself on visit from the cold north. The girl is my student. Now let us pass!"

"Yes, yes, Master Scholar. Right away," the guard said, bowed, and stepped aside to let them through.

As they passed beneath the white arch, there was a brief flicker of light, and then the air seemed fresher and cleaner despite the smells from the people, livestock, and goods around them. The sky seemed a little less overcast and the breeze less cold. Here the substrate was still mother-of-pearl and slightly sandy but without the mud and dirt of the lowest level. Thus, the streets and buildings were much cleaner. When they gazed over the edge of the nacre they could see the rickety rooftops and chimneys and streets and alleys in the stratum below. Fortunately, the distance was too high for its smells and smokes to reach them.

Dame Logan strode on, looking neither right nor left on her way up the gently sloping road. They passed only a few individuals, all clad in similar burgundy robes as the scientist. More carriages and wagons passed them than they saw in the lowest level, and these were pulled by mules or horses. No donkeys or goats here. Unlike the cramped and ramshackle half-timbered houses below, the buildings on this level were solid structures made of granite and sandstone with broad round arches bearing a solid capstone in the middle and windows in the same rounded shape with stained glass that was uneven and filled with bubbles.

"Who lives here?" Alexandra asked.

"Students and apprentices and scholars and scientists," Dame Logan replied. "These are the academies and colleges of Spiral. If you had grown up here, you would certainly have attended one of these."

Alexandra said nothing in reply. They followed the curve of the stratum uphill for a long time, the crunch of sand beneath their shoes and the passing coaches the only sound for a while. Droplets of sweat had started to collect on the bridge of Alexandra's nose. She was about to ask her grandmother for a break when the scientist stopped by a wide granite arch, and said, "Here we are."

THEY FOLLOWED DAME Logan through the arch into a large courtyard dominated by a complex maze of boxwood bushes cut to knee height. When the elf saw the hedge maze he wanted to run over to it and enter but was immediately stopped by a sharp look from Dame Logan. What's the point of having a maze if you can't run in it? the elf wondered. And anyone who failed to solve it could simply step over the hedge to get out.

The building they approached was a tall rectangle with a heavy front door flanked by snarling stone lions. Each half of the door held a solid brass ring at chest height. Dame Logan pulled at the ring, putting the weight of her whole body behind it. When the door finally gave she stumbled back against the elf.

"After the great fire," Dame Logan huffed, "all doors on the scholar stratum open outward for faster exit. You may just as well get used to it now."

Inside, the building was even larger than it looked from the outside. The center of the structure was dominated by a large atrium that stretched from the wine red tiles in the foyer to the ceiling five floors up. Narrow and steeply slanting ramps connected each floor. The entire back wall of the atrium consisted of glass divided into rectangles by solid black wooden frames. The sun had nearly managed to break through the thick clouds, and a few rays slanted onto the floor of the atrium. There were a noticeable draft and a hushed silence in the large room. Robe-clad figures moved along the mezzanines that lined the atrium and on the ramps between them.

The cat woke up and peeked her head out between the elf's lapels and clambered onto his shoulder. She sniffed the air and took in the entire space while her tail twitched. In the ceiling far above them, the glass orbs of a planetary display shone in the weak rays from the sun. The elf craned his neck and shaded his eyes with his hand. The display showed a blue orb at the center of the solar system while the other planets and sun circled that heavenly body.

"Well, what are we waiting for?" Dame Logan asked and started toward the first ramp. Alexandra and the elf followed her up into the building. On the top floor the old scientist followed the mezzanine for a short while before she entered one of the many corridors that led away from the atrium. They traversed these corridors for a long while. The elf suspected that some of the hallways they passed led back to the central court, but which ones he could not say as they twisted and turned too much. The floor in the corridors was so clean and thickly lacquered that it shone in the weak illumination from the skylights in the ceiling. The smooth brick walls held numbered wooden doors at regular intervals. Nothing else revealed what lay behind the barriers.

"These are the offices, studies, and enlightenment chambers of the top scholars in Spiral," Dame Logan said when the elf inquired about the rooms they passed.

"Enlightenment chambers?" Alexandra asked.

Dame Logan nodded.

"In order to become fully enlightened by the light of pure knowledge, some scholars brick themselves inside tiny cells. There they remain until they have become enlightened or die in the attempt."

The elf shuddered. What a terrible fate. "And how many do become enlightened by this method?" he asked.

"Not many," the scientist admitted. "Not many."

Finally Dame Logan stopped in front of one of the featureless doors. It looked just like the others. Its number read "574". The elf did not understand how the scientist had found the right corridor and door since the doors were not numbered in sequence or according to any other system he could recognize.

Dame Logan showed them all quickly inside and closed the barrier behind them. They were in a tall, narrow room with brick walls and the same gleaming floor as in the hallway. The room was lit by long, vertical windows that faced the courtyard outside, but most of the room lay in darkness due to its countless rows of open shelves. These were filled with glass jars, each topped by a circular glass lid with a round knob in the middle. The jars ranged in size from inkwell to bucket and were filled with liquid that varied from light yellow to bright orange to dark brown and everything in between. A strange, acrid smell filled the room. At first the fragrance smelled sweet and a little sour like fermented juice. But as they continued to breathe it, the scent turned sharp and cruel, stinging their eyes and throats like the driest of airs. It was no natural smell.

The elf had never felt anything like it, and after only a short while his eyes were running and his throat itching. Yet he felt even worse when he discovered what was in the jars. Each glass container held an animal, complete with fur or scales or feathers, its eyes, muzzle, whiskers, and paws intact, curled up and stuffed into the jar, then covered in colored liquid. As the shocked elf took in the glass containers, he saw a rat, a starfish, a serpent, an eagle, and a human hand. Each jar was someone's little grave.

The cat must have seen it, too, because she suddenly yowled, arched her back, and bristled her silky coat. The elf covered the cat's eyes and his own from the terrible sight, then pushed the cat back between his lapels. He imagined himself being dead and conserved in a jar like the animals and could not stand the thought.

"Do whatever it is you need to do here, scientist," the elf said. "And let's be on our way. Fast." The last word was drowned out in a terrible fit of dry coughing from the nauseating stench in the room.

Dame Logan laughed.

"I see you are enjoying the sights and smells of science," someone commented behind them. Through his tears the elf saw Dame Logan straighten her back and grin with her entire face.

"Dame Erengard!" Dame Logan yelled. "What a pleasure to see you!"

The old woman who apparently was Dame Erengard squinted a moment before she let out loud laughter.

"Dame Logan!" Dame Erengard shouted. "Is it really you? After all these years? I cannot believe my own eyes!"

The two women embraced each other like sisters.

"What brings you back here now?" Dame Erengard asked. She was as bald as a temple nun but wore similar gold-rimmed, crescent-shaped spectacles as Dame Logan.

"A fully completed model," Dame Logan replied. "My theorem is finally ready for presentation."

"Wonderful! " Dame Erengard exclaimed. "I knew this

day would come, however long it would take. Let's sit down for a moment." She clapped her hands, and from behind the nearest shelf, a student arrived. She nodded at Dame Erengard's commands, then returned a little later with a tray of halved and buttered breadrolls covered in slices of yellow cheese and cucumber and cups of strong black coffee. The food and beverage looked freshly made, but the scent of chemical death was too overpowering for Alexandra and the elf to eat. Instead, they watched Dame Logan and Dame Erengard help themselves to the breadrolls and coffee while they chatted and laughed.

After a small eternity the two scientists had finished their meal and catching-up. Dame Erengard gave Dame Logan a curious glance.

"I have a feeling I'm going to regret asking this, but I hope your visit means that your punishment has been annulled."

Dame Logan cleared her throat. "I'm just here to present my findings and attempt to have the annals rewritten," she said. "When that is done I will return to Canal. It's my home now."

When the elf heard that his heart sank in his chest. If they managed to avoid the Royal Guards in Spiral and Dame Logan fulfilled her task, he had no idea how to get them back to Canal. Logan had said she traveled by ship when she fled Spiral, but if they found no fare they would have to traverse the coast by foot. The elf did not want to take his chances with the forest again. It would be angry enough that they escaped the first time.

"The quicker I can do the presentation, the faster I will be out of your hair," Dame Logan said and gave her colleague a pointed look.

Dame Erengard merely nodded in reply. "I will call the assembly for an emergency meeting," she said. "But I'm afraid we can't do it before tomorrow morning at the earliest. Most of the Dames and Sirs have left for the day already."

Logan nodded. "That is fine. We can wait."

"Where are you staying tonight?" Dame Erengard asked, a little hesitantly.

The elf sensed that they would not be welcome in the scholar's abode despite her close friendship with Dame Logan. But he need not have worried. As usual, the scientist had a reply ready.

"We shall retreat to my old office," Dame Logan said. "I take it it's still here?"

"Yes, it is," the other scholar nodded. "It's not taken, but some people may have been using it as a storage facility and broom closet."

"Is it still possible to enter the room?" Dame Logan asked.

"It should be," Dame Erengard said.

DAME LOGAN THANKED her old friend for calling the assembly and for the meal and left Dame Erengard in the tall, narrow room. When they were back in the hallway the elf drew a deep sigh of relief. His eyes were still running, and his throat was too constricted and dry to speak; but at least they were out of the horrible smell.

Dame Logan sent him a glance full of humor and chuckled to herself. "You are clearly not a scholar, my friend," she said.

She then navigated them through the long, bewildering hallways, up one corridor, down the next, past seemingly randomly numbered barriers. Finally they stopped outside another featureless door whose number read "646". Dame Logan opened it slowly. The room was dark and narrow and filled with stacks of papers, books, and scrolls. The walls of the paper canyon reached all the way to the ceiling, which sat high above them and only had a few small, darkened skylights.

In a tin holder on the floor by the entrance stood the stub of a thick candle. Dame Logan bent down and produced an oblong brass object from her sleeves. From a small arm in the object protruded a circular black stone, which, when rolled with a snap of the fingers, produced a steady golden flame. She lit the candle and picked up the holder.

Alexandra, the elf, and the cat filed slowly into the canyon after the scientist while they tried not to disturb the precarious balance of the stacks in the paper canyon.

When Dame Logan stopped the elf turned toward her, expecting at least an insincere apology for the mess, but she didn't make one. Instead, she pulled some coarse wool blankets out from behind one of the stacks. Clouds of dust followed the motion of the old fabric.

"I used to sleep here a lot," Dame Logan said. "Quite comfortable floor, if I may say so myself." She handed Alexandra and the elf a blanket each. Lumps of dust clung to the thick fabric and seemed almost to be entwined in the threads of the itchy wool.

"Thank you," the elf said, courteously refraining from mentioning the mess.

Dame Logan swathed herself in an equally dust-ridden blanket and sat down on the floor, her joints popping from the motion. The light from the candle flickered warmly across her face. "Ahh, I'm back,. I'm finally back," she said, her eyes bright and eager. "My old office. So much has taken place here. It's a cradle of knowledge. Think about that when you sleep here tonight!"

The elf made a strained smile, sneezed, then laid down inside his blanket. The floor was hard, but at least they were indoors from the wind and rain. Dame Logan quenched the candle with a pinch of her fingers, and the room went dark.

The air smelled of dust, molded paper, and old age. Someone kicked over a small stack of books. It collapsed into the shelves hidden behind the stacks and pulled a few other heaps with it in a domino effect that fortunately toppled away from them. The elf was too tired to check who had caused the accident and rested his head on a small mound of yellowed scrolls and parchments in a corner. The cat wriggled herself under his blanket and nuzzled up against his throat. During the night the elf dreamed he was eating buttered bread rolls with slices of white cheese and cucumber in a room full of animals in jars while the dead creatures stared reproachfully down at him.

THE NEXT MORNING Dame Logan led them to the auditorium highest up in the Academy of Natural Sciences. This was a large semi-circular space and from the floor almost to the ceiling, dark benches in ascending tiers lined the room. The back of each bench served as a desk for the row immediately behind and above it. The benches were made from a polished dark wood that gleamed in the light from rows of long-armed brass chandeliers in the ceiling. The room reminded the elf of an amphitheater or a gladiator's ring. Only here the battles were of the intellect, not the body. Each tier of benches had a clear view of the lecturer's desk at the bottom of the room and the blackboard mounted on the wall behind the desk. From his seat at the top row, the elf felt like the room tilted slightly toward the desk and blackboard far below.

The auditorium started to fill. Old men and women with somber faces and burgundy robes filed through the doors on each side of the lecture hall one by one or two by two and sat down on the benches. Their clothes were wet from rain, so many of them slung their outer robes over the desk or the back of the bench. As a result, the air grew warm and humid and sleep-inducingly thick.

Thus, the elf's chin soon started bobbing toward his chest, and he had to fight to keep his eyes open. The cat was sleeping in his lap, blissfully unaware of his struggle and enviously free of the social convention that said one couldn't sleep whenever and wherever one liked to. Dame Logan and Alexandra had disappeared right after Dame Erengard opened the lecture hall for them. The scientist hadn't said where she was off to, but the elf assumed it was to gather her notes and prepare her presentation. The planetary display was now mounted in the ceiling above the desk but protected from view by its pewter dome.

This time the presentation started more dramatically. All the candles in the auditorium, except for those in the chandeliers at the far back, were quenched by students wielding small bronze bells on long sticks. Then the hood of the model lifted slowly to reveal the display lit by a single candle that shone through the stars from behind. At the sight of the starry sky, a murmur rose from the scholars in the auditorium. But it was not the display or its stars that was foremost on their minds, but its inventor.

"Is this Dame Logan's theorem?" someone asked loudly in the darkness.

"Shh!" said the elf who wanted to hear the presentation without interruptions.

"It looks like it. It must be!" someone else said.

"Is that old hen still alive?"

"Logan who?"

"Finally I get to see what all the ruckus has been about!"

When Dame Logan and Dame Erengard stepped out into the circle of wan light at the bottom of the tall auditorium a hush fell over the crowd. The elf imagined Spiral's best and brightest minds were busy trying to remember how Dame Logan's work had been interrupted and why she had left The Brilliance. Only a few whispered voices broke the silence.

"Is that her?"

"Yes, it is indeed Dame Logan!" the scholars whispered, not very quietly, since many of them were at an advanced age and a little hard of hearing.

"But wasn't she arrested for stealing some royal jewels?"

"No, she left the city!"

"As Director of the Board of the Academy of Natural Sciences of The Brilliance, the honored City of Spiral," Dame Erengard began, "I am pleased to introduce you to an old colleague and friend, greatly esteemed, deeply missed, and now finally able to return to us to present her grand theorem! This is a lecture that has been more than ten years in the making! Please welcome Dame Logan!"

"Hooray!" shouted the elf and clapped his hands. He was taking the chance that the impulse for consensus would work to his advantage. "Hooray for Dame Logan!" he continued. A small applause started tentatively in the auditorium. Then it spread and grew louder as more and more of Spiral's scholars, Dame Logan's old friends, colleagues, and acquaintances followed suit.

Dame Logan and Dame Erengard beamed and bowed to the audience, their eyes glittering in the light from the small illumination from the display. They looked like they were having the best night of their lives.

"Excuse me," a stern-looking, sinewy man who sat next to the elf said. The elf stood to let the man up from the bench and sat down again when he had left through the door behind them. Then the elf leaned forward, put his elbows on the smooth surface of the desk, and rested his chin on his hands to savor the lecture of the truth about the solar system.

THIS TIME DAME Logan described how she had discovered that the planets encircled the sun and not the Earth. She demonstrated that one of the planets went backward for a time before it seemingly turned to proceed forward once more in its orbit. This retrograde motion Dame Logan had not been able to explain until she theorized that it was only on Earth the planet seemed to go backward. If the vantage point was instead set at the sun, the planets always progressed in the direction they were supposed to. Thus, Dame Logan concluded, the Earth had to orbit the sun and not the other way around.

Dame Logan had several additional discoveries to support her grand theorem, including long lists of observations and measurements of the planets' orbits. The old scholars leaned over their desks while scribbling furiously on scrolls and consulting large leather-bound tomes they had brought with them. Some had detailed questions about what the discovery meant for the motion of the planets. Dame Logan followed up by drawing orbits on the blackboard behind her and presenting astronomical tables for the positions of the planets and the moon several years into the future. Yet more questions and arguments followed about these calculations and Dame Logan's methodology. The elf soon became lost in the sequence of explanations, and his eyes grew dry and weary. The air was warm and heavy, and his body was tired after several days' journey.

"Let's, for the sake of imagination, say that your theorem is correct, Dame Logan," a scholar with white hair and beard said and rose from his seat.

"Hear, hear," some of his colleagues shouted behind him. The rest of the audience was whispering and conferring with one another. The elf woke with a start and was about to add his voice to the chorus but refrained just in time as he realized these were protests uttered by Dame Logan's academic opponents.

"I do not imagine, Sir Valles. I theorize and confirm, and I am correct," Dame Logan replied at the bottom of the auditorium while she tilted her chin up.

"Well, for the sake of theory, then," Sir Valles said, "I'm sure you can do the leap in thought as well as most of us."

"Very well," Dame Logan said and pushed her glasses up. "What is it that you wish to say?"

"If your model is correct and the Earth is actually, however unbelievable and unnatural it sounds, orbiting the sun and not the other way around, why is it that we, here in the honored city of Spiral, always have the sun right above our heads, as if it is indeed always following the Earth like the trusty companion it is?"

"Hmph," Dame Logan said and tilted her chin up in as quick and stubborn motion as the cat had when she pulled at the reins in the forest. "Do you mean to imply that you take the side of the fables and the fairy tales of old that say the queen caught the sun in a length of twine and bound it forever to the tip of the utmost spire? Why, Sir Valles, I had never figured you for a fabulist."

"Never!" Sir Valles replied. "I am a scholar through and through and acknowledge only what my senses can test and my mind infer—not naive hearsay. But why is the sun always following the very tip of Spiral's structure? That is, after all, something we can all see for ourselves every day without the need to resort to tables of retrograde motion and complex calculations."

Dame Logan frowned and huffed again, but when she replied, she sounded less certain. "In all other places I have been," she began, "the sun moves differently than it does here. I have made several measurements in a great variety of regions. Since no one has examined the light at the tip of the utmost spire in situ, we do not really know what it actually is, and thus ..."

"What?" someone in the audience cried.

"Does she dare question the king and the royal family?"

"Who does she think she is?"

"Thus!" Dame Logan shouted at the depth of her voice to silence the yelling and waving scholars. "Thus, we cannot with absolute certainty say that the light at the spire is the same as the sun which is seen everywhere else!"

But this only served to create another wave of strong and indignant emotion among some scholars while others applauded and shouted "Hear, hear!" and "That's what we have been saying for decades!"

THE ELF TRIED hard to catch up on the debate, but the door behind him banged open. A row of guards in golden royal mail rushed through the narrow opening into the dark auditorium.

"There she is!" yelled a voice, quite unnecessarily, since Dame Logan was still standing in front of the lecturer's desk at the bottom of the room.

"Huh, what?" the elf said and sat up. His body was faster than his thoughts. He tucked the cat inside his robes, grabbed the heavy journal the old woman next to him had on the desk, and threw it at the incoming guards. Sheets of paper flew out into the narrow stairs that flanked the benches, creating a small avalanche of paper. In the darkness and chaos, several soldiers slid on sheets and fell on their bottoms.

"Fire!" yelled the elf. "Fire! Everyone, out! Get out!"

"Fire? Where?"

"What's going on?" the confused scholars cried. They were nevertheless getting up and quickly started to file into the stairs, inadvertently blocking the path for the guards.

The elf sprang up on the nearest desk, dodged the long arms of one of the Royal Guards, and made a long flapping leap to the nearest brass chandelier above. The brass arms shook terribly. All its candles shivered, but the chandelier held. The elf swung himself down the tall room to the master scholars at the bottom of the auditorium and dropped to the floor. The chandelier swung back so hard it crashed into the rear wall, showering the nearby guards with hot wax and embers. The impact snapped the chain that held the chandelier, and the whole object tumbled and rolled down the stairs, further impeding the progress of the guards.

"Stop them! Stop them!" the guards yelled.

"Fire! Fire!" shouted the scholars and pushed and shoved their way toward the exits. Some of the cloaks and robes that had been hung on the benches had caught fire, and the old fabrics flared up like tinder.

DAME LOGAN WAS standing in front of the lecturer's desk with her hands shading her eyes, staring out into the dark room from her lit spot.

The elf heard the sudden roar of flames that were taking serious hold of the room.

"Dame Logan!" shouted the elf. "We need to leave! Now!" He didn't wait for a reply but pushed the scientist toward the narrow door at the bottom of the stairs. Once she started moving, Alexandra followed, too. When Dame Logan spotted her granddaughter she woke from her panic.

"No! The display!" Dame Logan yelled. "We must save it!"

"It's too late!" the elf shouted. He grabbed the scientist's arm and pushed Alexandra in front of him. Remembering Dame Logan's words that all the doors at the Academy of Natural Sciences pointed outward, he towed them to the door. They fell through the opening and into the small antechamber where the lecturers made the last preparations before they entered the auditorium. Here the scholars could store their outer cloak and boots, as well as scrolls, maps, books, and other material that were to be used in their lecture. Chalk for the blackboard, sponges to wipe it with, candles for the chandeliers, plus a pewter pitcher and goblets to refresh the scholars during the intermission were stored in the bookcases that lined the little room.

The elf rushed up and shut the door, then pushed one of the bookcases in front of the barrier.

"Come on!" the elf said, and continued to pull the scientist and Alexandra with him.

THEY SLIPPED OUT into the seemingly endless corridors and ran for a long time, the sound of their feet echoing in the silence. They met no one—neither scholars nor guards—and saw no signs of fire—only the smell of smoke. Finally, Dame Logan led them to a dark, wooden stairwell that sat outside the building. They rushed down the stairs and into the outside garden. Dame Logan rose one hand in the air and bent over, wheezing and coughing. Giving the old scientist a little time to catch her breath, the elf turned back toward the squat building. Bright flames enveloped the top floor and dense smoke curled around the eaves like thick waves. The sound of glass breaking from the heat was audible.

He went over to Dame Logan. Her face had a peculiar greenish-grey hue, and she was still hunched over. "How are you doing?" the elf asked.

The old scientist just shook her head, still unable to say anything.

"Come on," the elf said. He took hold of Dame Logan's shoulder, bent, and lifted her up on his back. Then he ripped a hole in the sleeve of Alexandra's robe, put his wrist through the hole, and pulled her along with him.

THEY DISAPPEARED INTO the tall greenery of the academy's garden. It ended abruptly in an unprotected precipice that sat right above the tier below. From the height they were at now, near the gate to the third stratum, they could see the smoke-darkened, saddle-backed roofs of the city below and the harbor with all the boats and ships bobbing on the grey water of the bay. Past the mother-of-pearl docks of the harbor, they could even see the line of trees that marked the entrance to the deep forest.

Counting that not many people in the city below ever looked up for fear of getting a pail full of night soil in the face or that the academy garden was so high up that anyone there was a little speck against the sky, the elf followed the tier's sharp edge as it curved away from the academy. The grass and fern and moss dangled over the edge. Even a tiny stream fell into the air to the tier below. But the group's progress along the mother-of-pearl precipice was halted by a tall brick wall. As everything else in the garden, the wall simply ended at the edge of the precipice with no other boundary to the drop. But years of moisture and growth allowed some soil and grass to peek a little past each side of the wall.

The elf stopped and put Dame Logan down. She was still breathing hard and clutching her chest.

"Damn you," she groaned. "You're taking off years of my life."

The elf merely gave a short bow to the criticism before turning back at the wall to inspect it closer. Alexandra sat down in the wet grass and cried quietly.

The wall was easily one and a half times the height of a man. It was far from smooth and had numerous irregularities and dents and bumps in the surface. The elf knew he would easily be able to scale the wall, but he would not manage to get the scientist and the girl across that way, nor could he carry them across that height. But they had to move fast before reinforcements arrived and started to comb the Academy and its environs properly. The fire in the building and the physical distance for communication between the tiers seemed to have slowed down the guards for now.

"Stay there," the elf said and began to climb the wall. He only needed the tiniest of hand- and footholds to scale it. Even though he was wearing gold and purple slippers that ended in an elegant crest at the toe, which did not help the climbing, the surface of the brick wall was rough enough to make the elf pass with relative ease.

"Grandmother, grandmother, the elf is leaving us," Alexandra piped.

"No, I'm not," the elf whispered. "Just stay there and I will help you over to this side!"

The adjacent property was even more overgrown than the Academy garden. The grass had not been cut for years. Stout trees shaded the tall vegetation. Best of all, there were no guards in sight. Everything seemed quiet.

The elf took the gray cat out from his sash, put her on the ground, and gently petted her head. She purred and glanced up at him with blinking eyes before she sat down in the grass to wash herself, careless of her companions' plight. He moved to the end of the wall and peeked past it into the Academy garden.

"Here, my friends!" he hissed. Alexandra looked up and got to her feet, dragging her grandmother with her. Dame

Logan was now less green in the face—but scowling rather unhappily.

"Crawl slowly to the edge of the precipice as far as you can until the grass starts to give and then leap toward me," the elf said and stretched his arms out as far as he could. "I'll catch you."

Alexandra, fearless as most teenagers, did as she was asked. She managed to squeeze herself nearly fully past the edge of the wall and only had to fling herself into the elf's arms to get to the other side.

But then it was her grandmother's turn. She was both taller and heftier than the elf. But worst of all, she was stiff and afraid. "You are insane," Dame Logan muttered, shaking her head. "It will never work."

"Your granddaughter made it," the elf replied. "And she's almost as tall as you are. Just crawl out as far and as close to the wall as you can. Then jump toward me."

"No!" growled the scholar. "I'm an old woman, my bones ache, I have fifteen grandchildren, including the one who is with you now, I have just lost my life's work thanks to you, and there is no way I will fling myself over the precipice and into your arms!"

"Don't be ridiculous," said the elf. "Look how far over the edge the grass grows. And by the way, I was not the one who was hellbent to return to the place where I stole the royal treasures. I merely escorted you here."

At that the old scientist started to weep. Small tears trickled from her eyes and into the deep wrinkles in her face.

"Come now," said the elf. "I shall help you gain the display back even if I need to steal it from under the nose of the king himself."

Finally, Dame Logan sniffed and dabbed her eyes with the sleeves of her burgundy robe. "Be careful what you wish for," she sniffled. "I'm certain the king will have the orbs back once the fire has been put out."

"Won't the fire damage the orbs completely?" the elf asked.

The old scholar scoffed. "How do you think I gained the treasures in the first place? There was a sudden fire in the royal gem vault. No, a regular fire isn't hot enough to damage the pure minerals and brass alloy the display is made of. That's how I can light the sun sphere in the presentations."

The elf hadn't thought of that before. He realized that he had a lot more to learn about science and precious materials. "Come on, jump now," the elf said to have the old scientist dare the leap while her courage was up. He stretched out his hands.

Dame Logan nodded, then crawled on her hands and knees to the edge of the wall. There she crouched and stared into the empty space. "It's terribly far down," she muttered. An autumn breeze was blowing, cold enough to bite their ears and redden their cheeks.

"Don't think about that," said the elf. "Come now."

Dame Logan got to her feet, trembling, while she supported herself to the wall with one hand. Then she flung herself forward.

But Dame Logan hadn't aimed well enough for the other edge. She landed but immediately slid off grass on the other side of the wall. Quick as a striking snake, the elf grabbed hold of her, ripping the back of the scientist's dark robe. Dame Logan tumbled over the edge with a loud yell but stopped just before she pitched fully over.

The elf clutched Dame Logan and watched the old scientist scramble in the air with her leather-clad feet. Somehow, the motion helped, and the elf managed to grab the old scientist's leather belt. He took hold of it and pulled.

After much huffing and puffing and swearing and grunting, the old scientist finally got a knee over the edge so the elf could pull her away from the precipice. There they both lay in the grass for a while, panting and trying to get over the burning pain in their arms and shoulders and legs and knees.

***

"COME, COME. WE have to continue," the elf said after a few moments. "The guards must be searching all of the Academy buildings and grounds, thus we need to put as much distance between us and the Academy as fast as possible."

Alexandra looked fine, even a little excited, thought the elf. For her this was probably an adventure, challenging yet also exciting. For the old scientist, though, this was deadly serious. She had just lost everything: her life's work, her fortune (albeit acquired by unlawful means), and the chance to redeem her professional name.

Dame Logan now looked almost as aged and haggard as she had in the forest. The elf hoped she would be able to continue a little farther. The cat, on the other hand, looked as happy and calm as before. She probably didn't even consider herself a part of the recent crime, since she was, after all, a small animal. However, she was nothing but a little, loyal creature and remained perched on her master's shoulder, purring ever so slightly.

The small group stayed at the back of the very overgrown, dark garden and kept to the precipice. In the tall grass grew long ferns, hogweeds taller than the elf, and bright yellow birdsfoot trefoil flowers. Here and there, sharp stones jutted through the soft soil, and the knotted roots of pines crossed the ground. The air smelled strongly of earth and vegetation, and they even heard the hollow sound of a woodpecker's characteristic signal.

"What kind of place is this?" asked the elf. "Who set up a small forest in the scholar tier?"

"It's the Library of Virtues' garden," Dame Logan huffed. "Each year they get a decree from the Scholar Tier Architectural Committee to clean up their garden and cut down the trees that are hanging over the neighboring properties. And each year the old but stubborn prioress of the Library throws the missive into the huge fireplace in the kitchen."

The elf chuckled. What a quaint and wonderful city this was. The Brilliance did not turn out to be as dull and impersonal as he had thought.

"There surely will be another letter right away when both the Guards and the Architectural Committee realize that the untended garden was an asset for fugitive criminals," Dame Logan said drily.

"And will that make them clean up the yard?" the elf asked.

"Probably not," Dame Logan replied. "If anything, it will just make them stauncher in their resistance. Because what can the Committee really do? The Library gets its income from donations, not the king. In fact, he unwisely claimed the Library's uselessness since every Academy has its own private collection of books and scrolls. And the property has been the Library's for generations. All the Committee can do if it wants the garden cleaned up is to send in gardeners and workers themselves, something they obviously do not wish to do as it would cost them a large part of their yearly budget."

The elf whisper-laughed again. "No wonder they limit themselves to merely sending angry letters," he said.

They came to the end of the forested garden where another wall—this time in pale stone—barred their progress.

"Now what shall we do?" asked Dame Logan.

"We continue," the elf said. "They've had time to search the entire Academy and surrounding streets for us by now. Soon they will spread to search the garden and neighboring properties. We need to be long gone by then."

"All right," Dame Logan breathed. Fortunately, her chest pain seemed to be gone. She was no longer clutching her chest or breathing as hard as earlier. "The next garden and the following will take us closer to the upper gate. Is that where we want to go? Shouldn't we just descend to the lower city and catch a ship home?"

"That's what they expect us to do, to flee," the elf said. "They will probably check all outbound ships leaving tonight and tomorrow. The lower city is so large we could hide there until it is safer to get passage. However, they will never expect us to remain to try and get the display back."

Dame Logan shot the elf a sharp look. "That is folly!" she hissed. "We can't do that! All is lost. The best we can do is return to Canal and hope that our crime is not great enough for the city to extradite us."

"Do you really want to take that chance?" the elf asked.

The scientist's back sank a little. "What else can I do? I'm just an old woman ..." Her gray eyes started looking wet and red again.

"Is there any way we can get through the gate to the next tier?" he asked to distract the scientist.

Dame Logan thought for a brief moment, then shook her head. "Not unless we are accompanied by a Guard. They are the only ones who can pass through the gate to the Guardian Tier.

"Why didn't you say so first?" the elf asked. A plan was forming in his head.

"Because you didn't ask!" Dame Logan hissed and glared at the elf. "Oh no, you don't," she said. "Oh no, you don't!"

But it was too late. The elf bolted into the garden forest toward the street outside. He ran out in the middle of the busy road, a birdsfoot trefoil flower stuck in his hair, and yelled, "I found them! I found them! The criminals are here! Arrest them!"

A sizeable contingent of Royal Guards, their golden and white armor flashing in the sun immediately turned and apprehended the elf. After a brief chase they caught the fleeing scientist and her granddaughter, too. The three criminals were then securely chained and escorted through the Upper Clergy Gate and the Lower Guardian Gate to the Structure of Nominal Custody in the middle of the Guardian Tier.

SEVEN
THE GUARDIAN TIER

THE GUARDIAN TIER DIDN'T LOOK LIKE what the elf had expected at all. He had envisioned hulking stone giants in heavy armor and long swords flanking the central road glaring down at the passing people to make certain they didn't do or thought about doing anything wrong. Or grand statues of princes and generals on horses, their cloaks and hair blowing righteously in the wind of justice. Or white marble arches haughtily celebrating the military triumphs and cohesion of the Kingdom.

Instead, the Guardian Tier was clean and silent and subdued. As they were escorted along Circle Road, hands chained behind their backs and ankles shackled together in case any of them had flight in their heart, the mother-of-pearl beneath their feet was clean and white with only a few white gravel pebbles here and there. They saw no civilians in the main thoroughfare, only units of royal Guardians in their familiar white and gold armor and regular Guardians in dark green armor who were patrolling the streets in pairs.

In this stratum the buildings were white, featureless rectangles only a few floors in height or simple white domes with only a door in the front. Some of the structures were edged by a green lawn bounded by a low square-cut hedge or tall brick walls resembling the one at the Academy of Natural Sciences. There were no grand statues, frescoes, or arches. The elf was surprised.

The soldiers' faces were blank and passive. They didn't

look as if they had just caught a major criminal and her companions and were bringing them to jail. Instead, the royal Guardians looked like they were asleep.

"I hope you're happy now," Dame Logan growled in front of the elf. They had been chained together according to age in a display of generational crime and delinquency, no doubt to warn the populace against the heritability of crime and social irresponsibility; the old woman first, then the young man, and then girl.

The cat was nowhere to be seen, but the elf hoped she would return when things calmed down. "Well, getting arrested got us through the gate all right," the elf replied optimistically. "We needed that."

"Do we need to be executed, too?" the scientist asked. "Do you have any idea how fast decrees of beheading travel from the royal tier?"

"No," the elf said. "But I can imagine. Relax, we'll think up something."

Now even Alexandra began weeping.

THE EXPRESSIONLESS ROYAL Guards brought them midway between the Upper and Lower Judicial Gates in the middle of the tier. There the prisoners were brought into one of the featureless long buildings along Circle Road. This structure had small square windows all along its length. In the bright sun they gleamed like watchful eyes. A footpath of white gravel cut right through a thick lawn bounded by a painstakingly cut evergreen hedge. They were brought through stout obsidian doors into a low, wide hall paved with polished obsidian tiles. For a moment the sunlight slanted in through the open door, then shut heavily behind them.

The elf squinted into the semi-darkness, trying to see with his sun-blinded eyes. The black hall was completely silent. The walls were featureless grey tiles, and the air smelled dry and dead. The sterile, featureless surroundings frightened the elf more than a dark stone dungeon would have. He began to sweat. What kind of uncontrollable, unpredictable events had he set in motion now?

At least they can't take us into the basement, the elf thought. They were already on ground level with only the mother-of-pearl sheet of the Judicial Tier beneath them. But the elf was wrong. They were led down the silent obsidian hall between a row of short obsidian columns with rounded brass caps, then down a short staircase, through a brass gate, and into the basement.

This was the lowest floor of the building and hung over the precipice beneath the mother-of-pearl upon which the rest of the building stood. It was attached to its floor by strong iron clamps. Thus, no door led out of the basement except for the short obsidian stairs that went back up into the main building. Clearly, there was no escape except down.

THE GUARDS TOOK them into a small room covered by smooth obsidian, undid their chains while clasping their shoulders with strong hands in case they'd do something stupid, and shoved them inside a cage. The royal Guardians slammed the door to the cage shut and locked it behind them. It had a stained stone floor, and there was less than a hand's width between the bars. In the corner of the room was one more cage of the same size, but it was empty. In the center of one wall was a tall, narrow window about the same width as the bars of the cage.

"I'm surprised," the elf said after the Guardians had left and locked the door. "They really built a basement to this building and let it dangle over the precipice. Ingenious!"

"I suppose you're surprised they took us prisoner, too?" Dame Logan said, shooting a sour glance at the elf.

"Of course not!" the elf replied. "I intended to do that, to get us through the gate."

Dame Logan sighed. "Yes, and now all we need is to get

out of the strongest prison in Spiral." She slumped down on the dirty floor and buried her face in her hands. "Why, oh why, did I listen to you? We should have gotten away when we had the chance and run to the docks!"

"We ought to be glad we didn't because a storm is coming, and among the two ships that set off to Canal tonight, one will run onto land lured by shipwreckers in the storm and the other will go down with man and mice far out at sea."

"Well, I for one know how this will end, too!" Dame Logan said shrilly. "If you knew we'd end up here, you should have said so."

"But that was obvious," the elf protested. "We'd get caught and arrested, and that turned out to be right."

"I'm glad you're right about something," Dame Logan muttered.

They sat in silence for a good while. Then the elf asked, "How long do you think it will take them to douse the fire and retrieve the planetary models?"

Dame Logan looked sourly away, but after a while she had to reply, as the question interested her as well. "They will be busy putting out all of the flames tonight," she said. "They won't be able to start the search for the orbs until morning, when it gets light and the ashes have cooled a little."

"Perfect," the elf said.

Dame Logan looked sharply at him.

"Then there isn't much we can do until the orbs are found and brought back to the royal vault again."

"And why is that?" the scientist asked.

"Because we will steal them back."

Dame Logan sighed again, this time shaking her head, too. "Let's just try and get ourselves out of this particular vault first."

"Oh, we won't need to do a whole lot," the elf said. "We just need to open the window at the right time."

***

Two of the strongest forces in the world are longing and the belief that one needs something other than what one already has. Along Circle Road walked a little creature that up until then thought she had never needed anyone or anything else in her entire life. But at that moment longing burned in every hair of her dense coat, filled her entire awareness all the way out to the ends of her whiskers, down to the silent soles of her paws, and to the very tip of her long tail. It was annoying because it didn't go away.

With every push her paws made onto the smooth white mother-of-pearl, she wished she were back inside the gray robe covered by the gray cloak and surrounded by the reassuring scent of starlight and salt water. Her ears were cold when they didn't need to be, and her paws tired when they didn't have to. If she had still been in that comfortable space, curling her tail up to her snout, she would not have felt so chilly. Were she still sitting on the tall creature's shoulders, she wouldn't have had to dodge and duck and weave to get away from marching feet and stomping boots. Worst of all, if the hairless creature's warm hands had still been petting her, she would have felt much happier. She missed the uncat-like being, even as he had taken her away from her home and put hooves and mane on her for his own selfish transportation needs.

She had to find him again. She didn't know why he had lifted her out of the warm cave in the sash and placed her on the mother-of-pearl and walked away without once looking at her, but she felt deep inside her cat heart that it had not been without reason. Because who in their right mind abandons a cat? Especially a loyal one. She had done nothing wrong—not scratched or meowed or rebelled. She had done everything he had asked, and he had no reason to be unhappy with her. No, it must have had something to do with all the running and climbing and huffing and puffing they had done the last day. What a terrible and tiresome business that had been. She hoped it would soon be over so she could go back to sleeping inside the sash or sit on the warm shoulder in front of a good crackling fireplace.

Thus fueled by longing and a little bit of insult for having been abandoned without as much as a tousle on the head, the cat let her paws take her through the Upper Scholar Gate and Lower Guardian Gate and into the Judicial Tier.

She was distracted a few times by some sparrow chicks in a hedge, but the hedge was much too small and too neatly cut to serve as a hiding space for her, so she continued along the road. Once, a large man kicked after her while a black dog barked loudly. She hissed and spat at the man and his drooling companion and hurried on her way.

SHE COULDN'T SEE the elf anywhere, but it wasn't difficult to follow his scent. Since it was also mingled with that of the old woman and the girl's—a mixture of human sweat, old clothing, dried wheat gruel, and dust—it wasn't hard to follow at all.

The little grey cat walked and jumped and trotted along the road until she came to the long low prison building. There the scent trail stopped. She sniffed and scratched her claws a little on the lawn that led to the dark doors. The tall creature and his friends had definitely passed through here. But farther down the street she could not feel his scent. She glanced around. She had to investigate the box-shaped house more closely. But before doing so she urinated on the white gravel and kicked a few pebbles over it. She could just as well be done with that business now as later. Her belly growled. She really hoped the elf had something to eat when she found him. If not she'd meow and mewl until he did procure something for her.

She sniffed around the building in the closely cropped grass. It smelled faintly of humans but no one she knew—and the scents of soil, grass, fungi, earthworms, and bird shit. She followed the building all the way to the end and sniffed over the precipice. No, they had definitely not gone over there. Not even a cat would survive that fall.

But then she thought she heard a familiar voice. She listened a little more. The voice was vibrating and very faint.

Was that the old woman? She thought she recognized the sharp voice. And then the elf replied. The cat's ears shot up involuntarily, and she bent the tip of her tail with joy. There he was! If she could just find him, there would be warm hands, loving words, and something good to eat very soon.

But where was he? She sniffed and listened and looked around. Suddenly she discovered that there was a black wall below her, and it was from behind there that the elf and the old woman's voices came.

How to get down there? She sniffed and searched until she realized there was only one thing to do: jump down on the ledge. That would require some balance. She slid with her claws out down the dark wall, and just when her hind legs reached the ledge, she turned slightly in the air so that she came parallel with it. She landed on only three paws, one hind leg sliding off the ledge and almost taking her with it. She bore down with all her claws and managed to stop before she pitched over. Quickly gazing around to see if anyone had seen that rather clumsy performance, the cat licked her side a little, then sat up to continue on her way.

There was no one there. Only a few seagulls hovered on the wind some distance out from the ledge. They were busy quarreling, so she doubted they had seen her. Just in case, she clattered her teeth at them to make them know what they could expect if they disturbed her dangerous climb. Then she continued along the ledge. It was just wide enough for her paws and shoulders, but she had to suck her stomach in a little and mind her tail as she walked. The stupid elf, why did he run away? Now she had to work so hard to find him. Well, sucking in her gut was easy now that it was completely empty.

Fortunately, she heard the voices of the elf and the old woman clearly now. They were using the same tones they had used to each other for most of the trip. It sounded like kittens that had not yet been weaned. Disgraceful for adult creatures, she thought.

SHE WALKED CAREFULLY along the narrow stone edge, peeking in every tall, narrow window as she passed them. Not there, and not there either. Finally, she came to the right window where the voices were very loud. She could see the black top of the elf's hair. There she let out a loud and angry meow! She was cold and tired and needed petting and food!

"OH, THERE IS someone who wants to come inside," the elf smiled and turned toward the window. The gray cat was standing on her hind legs and scratching on the window.
"What?" Dame Logan said and turned, too.
"Hello, dear cat," the elf cooed. "Oh, that's a good kitty. How are you doing, my little friend?"
"That cat thinks she's a dog," murmured the scientist. "Let's just hope the wind doesn't blow her off the ledge."
"Yes, that is true," the elf said, staring at the cat. "I'll make her go hide in a moment."
As cat courtesy dictates lowering eyelids and looking away from the other in the conversation to signal harmony, it took a few seconds before the cat returned the elf's gaze, but once she did, swapping places with her took less than a second.

THE CAT GLANCED around. She was inside the room! As she had thought, it was warm and comfortable. The old person was with her, and the young one. But something wasn't right. She looked down at herself. And screamed. She dropped to all fours and began to run in circles while she meowed in despair. Then she started to wash herself in the hope that that would get rid of the itchy, restrictive clothes.

Outside on the ledge, the elf grinned as widely as the cat lips allowed him to. He purred at the cat to calm her and make it easier for her to accept the strange, new situation. There had been many uncomfortable surprises for her, things a cat could never imagine. He hoped his latest idea wouldn't scare her away for good.

"Don't panic, my little one," the elf said. "I'm just going to borrow your body for a few moments. Then you will have it back. Please sit down inside the cage and take it easy. I need my body when I come back."

"Ahhh!" yelled the cat, still licking and tugging at the sleeves of the outer layers of the elf's robe. But her ears were turned in the direction of the elf-now-cat, so he knew she was listening to him. "My fur is gone!" she meowed. "And my ears! And my tail!" The cat looked down at the body she now held, touched her ears, and twisted around to try and find her tail. Then she finally sat down. "This is a nightmare, and I'm dreaming!" the cat cried.

The elf whipped his newly acquired tail up and down once, then ran along the narrow beam to the last clamp. It was huge and pierced the mother-of-pearl that the prison cellar hung from. But from the clamp stretched a multitude of hairline cracks from strain and fatigue worn further by wind and rain.

Perfect, the elf thought with a small meow. He walked over the clamp, then squatted down, and peed on the cracks in the yellowed surface. He made certain that as much of the strongly concentrated feline urine as possible leaked into the cracks around the clamp. Then he jumped back down to the ledge, ran to the next clamp, repeated the process there, and continued to the next one. By the time the elf had urinated on the last clamp, wind started increasing in strength. Leaves and grass were flying about in the cold wind. A storm was approaching.

In order to switch back, the elf had to run back to the

window outside the cell and catch the eyes of the cat again. He sat down outside the window and peered in.

"Now you can have your body back," he meowed to the cat. She was slumping on the floor of the cage, but when she heard the elf, she raised her head and looked at him.

"This is the worst thing you have done to me," she said. "Turning me into a horse and then two horses was one thing, at least that was my own body. But this is just cruel. No fur, no ears, and no tail. How can you live with yourself?"

"Poor kitty," the elf said. He put his front paws on the smooth surface and raked along it with his claws, using his body weight to make the scratches as deep as possible.

"But we're still friends, right?"

"Mrf," said the cat, not very happy.

The elf laughed. "Come over to the window and you'll get your body back," he said.

The cat slid over to the side of the cage that was closest to the window. She squeezed her head out between the bars of the cage, which pulled roughly at the elf's ears. The elf wanted to tell her to be careful, but it was probably best she did it her own way.

Then with the agile nonchalance of cats and showing no fear of getting stuck between the bars, the cat began to squeeze out of the cage. Because as long as a cat gets her head and shoulders free, the rest of her body will fit through the same opening. Outside the window, the elf heard the clothes rip and winced.

"Be careful," the elf said, sweating in the cold wind.

"Why?" the cat said. She meowed in pain, but was so determined to get out of the cage she finally managed to squeeze through.

The elf cheered at her. The cat sat down in front of the window while she looked down at him with a pleased and expectant expression in her face.

"Be careful when you get out here," the elf said. "It's very windy, so you need to get back to the garden and seek shelter there. Things will start flying about soon."

"All right," said the cat. "I'll do that. Can I have my body back now?"

The elf nodded, then switched places with the cat. Then he doubled over on the floor.

"Are you all right?" Dame Logan asked from inside the cage.

"No!" the elf whimpered. "She nearly pulled the most sensitive parts of my body off!"

"Huh?" asked Logan. "You have been acting very strangely the last half hour. Are you sure you're all right?"

"Yes," the elf groaned. He delayed getting up a little bit longer. The right side of his head felt like it had been burned. And a part of his beautiful outer robe had been torn off. Well, it could have been worse, he thought. At least the cat had managed to get out of the cage a lot faster than he would have.

"If it pleases the gentleman, maybe he can try and open the cage for us now?" Dame Logan asked sarcastically.

"Oof, yes," the elf said. "Just one moment." He staggered to his feet and limped over to the cage door. Fortunately, it had just a small, simple lock. The Judiciaries must assume that even if prisoners somehow managed to get out of the cage, the sturdy door at the end of the room and past the Guards upstairs would be a whole other question.

"Here, use this," Dame Logan said and handed the elf a thin, long metal object. It was a hairpin decorated with glittering emeralds.

"How do I use this?" the elf asked

Dame Logan rolled her eyes. "Stick the thin end into the lock slowly and try to lift all the inner parts of the lock with it. Feel around for the lock mechanism and try to catch it with the end."

The elf did as the scientist had instructed and pushed the hairpin into the lock and tried to feel around inside. It was all made more difficult from the prison shaking slightly, as if heavy feet were crossing the floor above. After a bit of fiddling, the lock clicked open, and the cage door slid ajar.

"Come on," Dame Logan said to Alexandra, who had been sleeping most of the time because "it was boring" there. The scientist helped her granddaughter out of the cage and finally left the confinement himself. The elf closed the door of the cage shut.

BUT NOW THE entire room was vibrating, and not only from their footfalls on the floor. Heavy gusts of wind hit the soaring basement on the broadside. Through the narrow window they could see that dark clouds were smothering the sky. Small objects—such as leaves, branches, even pebbles— flew around in the air. A sharp blue light ripped across the heavens and split into many small tears. The thunder clap that followed rolled across the bay, vibrating the hanging prison even more.

"Stand here and keep hold of the cage," the elf said. "Whatever you do, don't let go! And stay away from the window!"

The scientist and her granddaughter didn't say anything but squatted down by the short end of the cage. Their eyes turned large and moist as the whole room started to shake as the storm increased its power.

A hail of pebbles hit the window. Both Dame Logan and Alexandra screamed and ducked their heads. The elf pushed them farther into the room, as far away from the window as they could get. Then a blast of wind and pebbles smashed the window into a thousand gleaming pieces. The storm sucked some of the shards into itself, but the rest fell like sharp rain over the cages.

Alexandra and Dame Logan screamed again. An icy wind filled the room and spat needling drops of sleet on them. It whipped their hair and clothes, as if it wanted to pull them out of the open gap. The prison's elevation gave a frightening panoramic view of the raging nature. Lightning shot down from the heavens right past them. The flash was so strong and so close it blinded them momentarily. The thunder clap followed immediately, shook the room, and made their ears ring.

"Tie your clothes tightly around you!" yelled the elf and pulled at his sash. "And be prepared. We need to leave in a few minutes!"

If Dame Logan and Alexandra replied, it was drowned out by the din of the storm.

THE WIND WAS now constantly shaking the prison from side to side and up and down. The floor and walls and roof creaked like a ship in a hurricane and trembled with teeth-chattering strength. Even the heavy cages in their cell bounced up and down, so they climbed quickly on top of them and hung on as best they could.

The air was swirling so violently inside the low room it was hard to breathe because the storm pushed the air they were about to exhale back down their throats, making it feel like they were choking. The wind was so cold it brought tears to their eyes and bit their hands and ears. The shrieking and wailing and roaring and growling of the storm was now so loud they could not hear each other over the noise, and they were thrown about by the tremors of the room. It felt like the world was going to end.

The elf clung to the cage as it bounced with the potent rage of the storm, squeezed his eyes shut, and hung on with all his might. He tried to think of calm seas and blue skies, but it was hard when it felt as if the entire world was being thrown back and forth. He wondered if he had overdone it by loosening the attachments of all the clamps.

IT FELT LIKE something hit the prison cellar. A loud crunching noise tore through the structure and the sound of something snapping, which made the whole prison cellar tilt slightly. Dame Logan and Alexandra screamed.

That was the first one, the elf thought. He couldn't quite make out from the sloping of the room which clamp had gone, but it was probably one on the side of the structure most exposed to the storm. It might be a question of time before others gave way, too.

And they did in rapid succession. At the next gut-shaking thunder clap and vibrations, which made the hanging prison shake and dance. Then followed two loud noises that sounded like explosions. It felt like the prison was falling into the abyss, but it stopped after a second and left the cage hanging at a steep angle. The cage slid along the floor and crashed into the wall at the bottom of the tilt.

"Ahh!" the elf shouted, but his yell was cut short by the air that was knocked out of him when the cage hit the wall. That made the damned thing almost topple over, but the elf crawled lightning fast over to the other side and stabilized the weight. He just prayed that the scientist and girl wouldn't faint from fear.

Dame Logan was screaming things the storm and vibrations drowned out. Alexandra had stopped yelling and was just taking in everything that happened with large, round eyes.

It felt like the storm took hold of the prison and was about to hurl it into the bay. But some of the clamps were still holding onto the mother-of-pearl above, so the only thing the wind could do was turn the prison in its place. With a dizzying shake and rattle, it shifted until it slammed into the edge of the stratum.

That was what the elf had been hoping for. He took hold of Dame Logan, heaved her onto his back, and pulled at Alexandra's arm. He knew he had to be fast and move before the next violent gust of wind hit the prison because that could be the last time.

***

THE ELF MOVED for the window with Dame Logan first. It took a few seconds for the old scientist to realize that she had left the top of the cage, but when she did, she began to flail and bang the elf on his back. Fortunately, when the elf squeezed himself out of the window, back first, Dame Logan fainted and went still.

"Stay there and hang on!" the elf yelled to Alexandra. She didn't respond but hunched down right inside the window, away from the direct wind.

Outside, tree branches, roof panes, wood planks, what looked like the remnants of a sail, and other fairly large, heavy objects were flying through the air. The elf stood on his toes on the ledge and pushed Dame Logan up onto the cracked mother-of-pearl. He gave the unconscious scientist a good push so she rolled farther onto the white surface. Then holding onto the uneven surface of the stratum edge, he bent down, took hold of Alexandra, and lifted her up on his shoulders. From there she could climb up on the ledge, where she crawled farther in, and helped the elf drag himself up.

Panting and huffing with every muscle in his body feeling like it was on fire, the elf stumbled across the Judiciary Garden and into the next property, crossed its closely cropped lawn, and went farther into the next area. There someone had painstakingly planned, grown, and cut a hedge maze. Since the height of the maze only reached to his thighs, it wasn't difficult to navigate. But the elf, stumbling under his burden, did not have the strength or flexibility left in his joints to step over the low hedge. Instead, he followed the artificial intricacies of the maze until they came to a corner. There the elf's knees gave way. He rolled the scientist beneath the hedge, and the girl followed suit. The hedge's foliage did not reach all the way to the ground but had been cut a foot above the soil, so there was room enough to stay beneath the hedge and be fairly sheltered from the buffeting wind and the icy sleet, as well as any watchful eyes from the main thoroughfare.

The elf stretched slowly, trying to tease blood back into

his limbs. I'll be sore in the morning, he thought. For the future he'd best avoid physical excesses like this, but their imprisonment had, after all, been his fault entirely. He startled as a small shadow leaped over the nearest maze wall and headed directly toward him, but then smiled broadly.

"Oh, my dear!" whispered the elf and held out his hands. It was of course the gray cat, who had been hiding from the storm inside a small nook in the outer wall of the Judiciary building while she waited for them to escape. The warm, little creature stood on the elf's folded arms, supported herself on his chest, and licked his face with her rough tongue. The elf laughed and hugged the cat. Then he sat down by the hedge and rolled in beneath it with the cat safely on his belly.

However, unbeknownst to the elf and the rest of Spiral, the storm had, in its rage and gusting, unearthed a monster. It had been sleeping in the earth for a long time in close proximity to the humans who lived across the bay. There it had hidden and spread itself in the bodies of the grunting livestock that trod its ground every day and searched in the dark dirt with their pink snouts after roots, seed, rotted plants, and fruit. The monster had grown strong inside the pigs before it moved temporarily to the white and brown and black chickens that lived among the pigs and pecked their droppings in search for seeds, grubs, larvae, beetles, and leftover food. This foray had almost cost the brewing monster its existence, as most of the hens had not been receptive to it and died within hours of contracting the epidemic. But a few of the chickens survived long enough for the monster to adjust to the new organisms and spread, affording it the ability to infest both chickens and pigs before it returned to the pink diggers and gave rise to a whole new version of itself. One that had no problems invading the long pigs that lived near heaven in the tall heap across the bay.

Then the storm came and kicked up mud and dirt and

soil and plants and fences and chicken and bird coops and infested hay and droppings. Most of this fell back down on the farms and villages outside the city. Another large part fell impotently and spent into the dark waters of the bay. But the tiniest drops of infested mud, dirt, and water still found their way across to the spiral of mother-of-pearl. There it beat against every window and door and wall until it was let in by at least a few people when they had to leave their safe havens to visit the outhouse, fetch more firewood to keep the heat going, or when they dueled each other on top of the balustrade of a marble staircase because that seemed the most dramatic and appropriate thing to do in a storm.

Thus, the monster found its way into every tier of the white spiral from the lowest to the highest. There it sat on the hands and palms of more and more people to penetrate their noses, throats, and lungs. Whenever these people talked with one of their fellow citizens the monster spread in the form of tiny, invisible droplets that landed on the hands and face of the next person.

THE ELF SLEPT beneath the hedge with the gray cat on his belly. He dreamed about the cold coast, the little hut, and the endless beach. The sea there would be carrying broken ice in the winter and remain cold in the summer, but the sand would be soft and the sun glitter the surface like diamonds. From far away he could feel his body shiver and heard thunder barrel across the sky. It was not day yet, but a grey had started to blossom at the edge of the bay. He remembered they were only two gardens away from their original prison. If they were to move, this would be a good time.

The elf drew his breath sharply to wake further and tried to sit up. Instead, he scraped his forehead on the twigs and leaves he was lying under in the hedge maze. The cat jumped down from his belly with an annoyed meow and started her morning wash. (The elf looked at her with a smile. It was fascinating how cats seemed to be at home in almost any situation and were always graceful no matter what happened. He really admired that in cats.)

With a sigh and shiver, the elf rolled sideways out from under the hedge and sat up. The ground was soaked, so he got a cold wet spot in the seat of his robes. How annoying! He crouched against the hedge and peeked above the almost completely straight line of the hedge.

In the shivering gray morning Circle Road and the gardens along it were empty. The wind was still strong, and leaves, branches, and even parts of bushes were still roiling around in the gale. The air smelled of mud and feces. The elf wrinkled his nose. What a horrible stench! The hurricane must have overturned the rotting clay on the shores of the bay or destroyed several chicken coops in the lowest stratum by the smell of it. Frowning, the elf took one of his long scarves—a cobalt colored one—and tied it over his head and face so that only his eyes peeked out from between the soft fabric.

The city looked dead, but that was only an illusion. Down in the strata below, golden lights filled the windows of a building here and there. The sound of a barking dog floated up from the bottom tier. Out in the bay the masts and sails of several ships stuck out of the frothy water while others stood nose-first in the waves. The storm had even blown a few huts and houses on the docks into the bay. The half-timbered walls and buckling roofs lay collapsed and crumbled like card houses in the agitated water. On the far shore was a substantial hole in the row of trees that bordered the forest. A huge ash tree had fallen into a sharply slanted barn roof and opened up a wide hole.

In the present tier, mud and dirt blackened the street. Even the pristinely white Judiciary buildings were soiled with rain-borne mud and dead leaves. The prison basement now hung askance, barely attached to the rest of the prison structure.

When the elf saw that, he laughed. "Did I do that?" he chuckled. The cat purred and rubbed her side against his ankles. "We did, didn't we?" the elf asked the cat and hunched down to pet her.

"What?" Dame Logan said and sat up to her indignant surprise of the branches and leaves she was lying under.

"Who said that?" Alexandra muttered and opened her eyes.

"Are we in the clear?" Dame Logan hissed, crouching behind the hedge.

"Seems so," the elf muttered. He looked at the scientist and the girl. Their clothes were wet and rumpled and a little torn, but they were all in one piece. The girl even seemed sprightly, and the scientist seemed to have regained her focus.

"We broke out of jail!" Alexandra said, looking more excited at that thought than the elf thought she should.

"Indeed, we did," the elf said. "But we need to get farther away from the prison before we can consider ourselves safe."

"Let's do it!" said the girl and jumped up.

Even Dame Logan laughed. "I cannot believe it," she said. "I'm cold and hungry and thirsty, but damn, we got out of that prison." The scientist set her jaw and straightened her back, now looking about thirty years younger.

"You're not angry?" the elf asked.

Dame Logan laughed again. "Of course I am, but this whole escapade reminds me of my youth! I feel young again!"

The elf laughed. So that was the effect adversity, delinquency, and destruction had on old scientists and young women, he thought. No wonder a life of crime was heritable.

"Are you ready to continue?" the elf asked.

Both the scientist and the girl nodded.

"But to where?" Dame Logan asked.

"There," the elf said and pointed.

IT WAS A surprising sight. The autumn-barren branches of a massive honeysuckle plant had been blown over the edge of the tier above by the storm along with a monstrous statue and some large masonry that lay scattered on the white gravel in the next garden. The honeysuckle branches were so long they were dangling just a few feet above the wing of the overturned statue. As if regretting the long fall that had separated its head from its body and broken one of its long wings, the face of the monster statue grimaced from its place on the soiled, cracked mother-of-pearl.

The three fugitives crouched behind the hedge maze, then slunk across the low greenery and into the garden beyond. There they snuck from cone-shaped bush to cone-shaped bush of decorative greenery until they stood at the statue's body that lay sideways and cracked. The elf let the girl and the scientist clamber up in front of him onto the monstrous wing and over to the lowest part of the honeysuckle vines that hung suspended above them. The branches were brown and stiff and almost as wide and solid as tree trunks. Only at the very edges was the wood soft and green and budding with next year's heavily perfumed flowers.

The elf asked Dame Logan and Alexandra to stand back a little and pulled at the branches—first softly and then harder. Then he put his entire weight on the vines. The wall of branches swung and moved but did not budge. He let Alexandra hang onto the vines and then the scientist. When they had put their full weights on the plant the elf pulled at the branches a few more times before he suspending himself from it. It seemed to hold.

"This plant should be able to take the weight of all three of us," the elf said.

"We're going all the way up there?" Alexandra asked and craned her neck.

"Yes, indeed," the elf said. "Try not to fall down. If you get tired on the way, let me know, and I will help you. When you get to the top climb up and hide as best you can."

"Will you help me, too, if I get tired?" Dame Logan grinned.

The elf scoffed. "No, because you're a young woman again, so I wager you won't even be tired from the climb."

Dame Logan laughed. When Alexandra took hold of the lowest branches and began to climb she promptly followed.

***

IT WAS A longer climb than the elf had thought. The smooth mother-of-pearl face of the stratum above didn't look like it was that far away. But when the path was a vertical climb that exceeded the height of more than twenty men, it was slightly different.

About half-way up, Alexandra made the mistake of looking down. "I can see really far out from here!" she shouted down at her grandmother. Fortunately, the wind was still high and masked her voice so Dame Logan couldn't hear her and make the same mistake.

"No, don't," Dame Logan yelled. "Keep looking upward!"

"Ahh!" Alexandra shouted as she saw how far it was to the ground. "Grandmother!"

"I told you not to look down," Dame Logan growled, but climbed faster. Alexandra was now clinging to the vine and wasn't making any more progress.

"Keep moving," Dame Logan said. "Let's see if you can get there faster than I can."

Alexandra shook her head and squeezed her eyes. "I can't!" she cried. "We're all going to die!"

"Pish pash!" Dame Logan said. "We didn't die when we were thrown around inside the prison, and we didn't die when we climbed out of it. I don't intend to start dying now, and neither do you. Now climb along!"

The girl hesitated but then started climbing slowly and carefully.

"What's up there, anyway?" the elf asked. "Any idea?"

"Heaven," Dame Logan puffed.

Eight

Heaven

EXHAUSTED, THE ELF SLAMMED ONE HAND on the rain-slick mother-of-pearl edge and heaved himself up.

"Meow," the cat said inside the elf's robes as she startled from the sudden movement and noise.

"Sorry," panted the elf and stood to take in the new surroundings.

He was awestruck.

On the top tier the sky was tall and blue with pure white good-weather clouds, even as the rain poured down. From the center of the sky at the very tip of the great twisting shell that was Spiral blazed a bright golden light that seemed as strong as the sun. Or maybe that actually was the sun attached to the spire at the height of the city. Directly beneath the spire, but far below it, sat a cathedral-like building with a sharply slanting roof, dark walls, soaring, narrow buttresses, and enormous stained glass windows with intricately curling whorls and loops and patterns in all hues possible to create in glass. The stained glass windows ended in high, thin arches and looked to be the height of several ordinary buildings.

This structure sat on top of and seemed to have melded together with a fortress-like building below. The fortress counted four broad watchtowers with dark roofs, square crenellations, and banners flying from the high walls. It rested on countless other structures beneath it: castles with seemingly endless rows of rectangular windows, strongholds, mansions, and estates with sharp roofs and gleaming windows, all looking like they had been melted or merged together. In this lump of mansions and fortresses and keeps, green dots of lawns and trees were visible here and there with even a few colonnades and arches visible. They could even spot white figures in some of the gardens—statues or fountains or other forms of decoration.

Even though the entire structure looked like it had grown together, there was no system as to how the buildings were attached to one another or whether their architectural style suited one another. Many buildings ended abruptly into another, had simply bisected the neighbor, or looked as if it had been squashed together. Yet others seemed to grow out of other buildings or had been trapped in the maws of their doors or enormous windows.

The entire conglomerate rose like a dark, jagged mound from the middle of the stratum that they now found themselves on. The flat expanse was covered in tall grass. Above them, in the blazing blue sky, the orb at the top of Spiral shone like the sun.

UPON SEEING THE top tier of Spiral, Dame Logan swept the loose hair from her bun away with one hand, making white wisps of hair standing almost horizontally out from her head. She bent her neck reverently with the look of a young novice stepping into an academy for the first time. The elf found the scientist's reaction strange and a little annoying. Fortunately, Alexandra had less appreciation for Spiral's elite. Instead of bowing, she exclaimed, "Oh!"

"Don't worry," the elf whispered to Dame Logan. "We have nothing, more or less, to fear here than we did in the lower tiers. No one knows we're here, and even the rulers that live here are creatures such as us."

At that Dame Logan seemed to wake and shook her head. "Yes, yes, you're right, of course," she said. "Absolutely." She removed the clasp that held her bun together, collected and pulled her hair back into the bun; but her hands shook a little.

"Let's get out of this rain and find something to eat," the elf said and started walking.

As they drew closer to the mass of buildings in the middle of the stratum, they spotted a broad wooden door with a black iron handle that sat in a slanting wall close to the grass. With a quick determined stride the elf headed straight for the door. Here and there the grass was soiled by heaps of horse manure and bore crescent scars from shoed horses. There were apparently riders on the circular field, but they would be easy to spot across the flat expanse. The elf nevertheless began to run as fast as he could, hoping that no one would peek out from the lump of buildings and see them against the green.

At the door they stopped, out of breath from the quick run. The elf took hold of the black cast-iron handle and pulled the door open. Dame Logan and Alexandra filed inside. The elf closed the door quickly behind them.

"UGH. WHAT KIND of place is this?" Alexandra asked. The room was completely dark, and they were standing ankle-deep in cold water. They heard dripping from several places around them.

"Don't let me down!" the cat yowled from her perch on the elf's shoulder.

"I won't, of course," the elf said. "You are safe here."

Dame Logan cupped her hands together, and a small yellow flame lit up from a small brass rectangle that had a black stone sitting on a brass arm. The device produced a small flickering illumination.

"Good," said the elf. "Now we can continue." His eyes needed time to adjust to the low light, but he didn't have the patience to stand still. He felt about in front of him to start moving as soon as possible. His hands met something dusty and smooth like a round bowl placed upside down. He lifted the object up to his face to take a closer look, only to stare into the empty black eye sockets of a human skull.

"Aah!" the elf yelled and tossed the skull away. It clattered along the wall and splashed into the water.

"Aaaahhh!" Alexandra and Dame Logan shouted in response.

"What was that?" Alexandra whimpered.

"Just ... just a skull," the elf stuttered and wiped his brow.

"You need to learn to look before you leap, or rather, see before you grope," Dame Logan said.

Finally their eyes had adjusted enough to the weak light so they could examine their surroundings. They were hemmed in on three sides by dark walls lined with black crescent-shaped holes. On the flooded floor sat several large stone sarcophagi—gray and ancient and pockmarked, all inscriptions on their lids faded by time and water. Beyond the small circle of Dame Logan's light, they could see the room narrowing into a tunnel that continued into the darkness.

"Oh, gods," the elf said. "A burial chamber."

"Haunted!" Alexandra chuckled.

"Please don't say that," gasped the elf.

"Oh, shut up, the both of you," Dame Logan said, giving them a stern look, as if they were misbehaving children. "We're not very likely to meet any ghosts because they are all dead!"

"Well, I was not the one who bowed to royals I've not yet met," the elf muttered sourly.

"That was something entirely different," Dame Logan hissed.

"Come on," Alexandra said and continued farther into the catacombs.

***

The walls were covered with bones of all shapes and sizes from the largest femurs to the smallest finger bones. The macabre material was whole and unmodified and pieced together like mosaic tiles into bands, wreaths, bows, arches, and other decorative patterns on the walls. In other places skulls had been placed together in neat stacks alongside pyramids and cones of other bones.

"Oh, look," the elf said. "Take one piece from each stack to form for a full skeleton."

"What a sad, sad fate," Dame Logan commented on the macabre displays. "Who would want to end up as wall decoration?"

"At least then they're pleasurable—even in death," the elf smiled.

Alexandra chuckled.

"Ooff," huffed Dame Logan and continued through the rotten water while she held the light high to see the way.

The whole place reeked of death. Mercifully, it was the smell of slowly rotting bones and not the stench of decomposing flesh. Mixed with this was the scent of clothes, paper, leather, and wood that disintegrated slowly in the cold and damp. Some corpses had been buried with various implements, and in most cases those items took a longer time to vanish than the worms, rats, flies, and beetles needed to rid the bodies of their meat.

They walked through dank, dark corridors decorated with the remains of the dead. At first the stench was overwhelming, but after a while they could breathe almost normally. Fortunately, the corridors seemed to slant upward and turned drier as they proceeded farther into the catacombs. The water shrunk to puddles on the dusty floor that were easy to circumvent.

In the great darkness and dead silence, it was impossible to say how long they continued. Here and there the walls glowed a ghostly green or blue from phosphorescent mold and lichen that crept along the stone, but for the most part it was as dark as a proper grave. Occasionally the tunnels ended in decrepit, crumbling stairs paved with the same small, often cracked flagstones as the catacomb tunnels, and having broad, low banisters. Each time they found a staircase they followed it up as far as possible in the hope of eventually reaching the lower floors of the lump of buildings overhead.

"I really wasn't expecting the nobles and royals to live on top of their dead ancestors," the elf sighed. He was thirsty, and his feet were hurting.

"Oh, but all nobles have a burial crypt or a mausoleum in their mansion," Dame Logan said. "It's tradition."

"But still ..." the elf said. "It's uncanny, and the smell must reach the floors above, too."

"It definitely does," Dame Logan said. "But there's so much there to mask the smell with: perfumes, powders, oils, flowers, fabrics, food." The scientist smiled, clearly recalling something pleasurable.

FINALLY, THEY CAME to a flight of very wide stairs. Most of the steps were still whole, as was the broad banister. The flagstones were covered by sand, grit, and dust like the catacombs below, but here more of them were unbroken. They could feel a cold draft flowing down from the stairs and climbed them quickly.

The stairs ended in an enormous dark room lit only by a huge yellow moon in the sky that shone in on the dirty, cracked floor through a row of impossibly tall, narrow windows framed in corroded brass. The dusty floor stretched into the darkness while the light of the moon was so bright they could see walls of the sprawling castle-mound above and the circular expanse of green below them.

"Finally out of the catacombs!" Alexandra exclaimed and headed for the windows.

"Wait, where are you going?" the elf asked and caught hold of her sleeve. "What if someone sees you?"

Alexandra scowled and pulled away from the elf. "I just need some fresh air after those smelly catacombs!"

"All right, but be quick about it," the elf whispered.

A long row of tall windows loomed above them. Each window consisted of panes of stained glass that sat pair-wise in a thin frame of golden metal—each twenty panes in height, including the arched ones at the top. The elf approached the nearest window. It started at shoulder height on the wall with each pane both taller and wider than an adult.

Farther down the row, one of the lower panes in another window had been blown in by wind and rain. Alexandra hurried over to the hole and noisily inhaled the fresh air.

"Me, too," Dame Logan said. "The stench in the tunnels made me quite queasy."

Now that the elf thought about it, he was a little nauseous, too.

All three of them stood in front of the broken window, deeply inhaling the cool air from outside. They had a panoramic view of the slopes of the enormous melded-together castles. They could make out several buildings that were integrated in the whole and a few gardens, yet saw no lights in any of the multitude of windows that gleamed in the moonlight.

"Do any of you see any lights?" Dame Logan asked.

"No," Alexandra replied. "It's all dark. How creepy."

"Maybe they are all asleep for the night?" the elf suggested.

"They probably are," Dame Logan said with a strange expression on her face that the elf couldn't quite interpret.

"There, look," Alexandra said and pointed at a spot far above them in the huge structure. A faint orange light was visible, flickering weakly behind dark glass.

"So there are people here, after all," Dame Logan muttered.

***

They continued through the hall, searching for a way farther up into the mass of buildings. The full moon cast a silver light onto the cracked floor. A draft from below brought with it the stench of the catacombs. The long room ended in a pair of elegant white doors with gilded moldwork surrounding the carved panes. Flanking the doors were white marble columns veined with gold. The wall above the doors had been painted the bright blue of a sunny summer's day; but the color was blistering and peeling, and mounds of fallen paint flakes had collected on the floor. Higher up on the wall they could make out white clouds, chubby baby angels flitting through the sky, men and women draped in robes and scarves of bright colors dancing in forests, under the moon, or in white marbled cities with rows of golden colonnades. These were scenes of an idealized existence, but time had faded most of the beaming faces and cavorting bodies.

Dame Logan reached for the golden handle of the door while she lifted the light high. Now they saw that the handle was shaped like a slender hand ready to be shaken in greeting. The artisan had carved gloves onto the hands. They were buttoned on the side, and the middle finger had a ring shaped like a bird's-foot-trefoil flower. As the scientist pushed the handle down, a crack and then a rumbling noise shook the entire wall.

"Watch out!" Alexandra yelled, pulling her grandmother away from the door. The elf jumped in shock and backed away, too. A landslide of wood, masonry, and small rocks burst the golden door, ripping it off the hinges and leaving it hanging to one side. With a deep rumble something very heavy scraped against the wall, then settled with a slowing crunch. Through the half-choked opening a puff of dust billowed, stinking of stone, soil, and old bones.

"The building must be moving from the weight of the structures above it," Dame Logan concluded.

With the door at that end of the room irrevocably closed, they followed the inner wall back into the darkness to see if it held any doors. This wall was covered with glass panes in the same size and style as the windows on the outer wall, but these panes had been leaded in the back, creating a wall of window-shaped mirrors. Two-thirds along the length of the room they saw something large and gleaming on the floor. They stopped and squinted into the darkness. Parts of the large object moved slightly in the cool air, and the sound of tinkling reached them. They moved slowly closer to the glittering heap.

The enormous crystal chandelier that had ended its days on the floor of the dark hall consisted of thousands of drop-shaped prisms the size of a grown person's hand. The chandelier itself was taller than four adults but had been twisted and bent in the impact. Beneath it the parquet had cracked and was strewn with glittering shards. The thousands of crystals still left on the chandelier glittered even in the faint moonlight from the windows. The prisms were suspended from curving golden arms attached to a long spindle-shaped body covered with a tube of patterned crystalline glass. The ends of each arm ended in a golden cup the size of a vase. From several of the cups protruded still broad white candles while others had fallen to the floor.

The elf gazed slowly upward. In the darkness of the high-vaulted ceiling, he could just make out a row of similar chandeliers going down the length of the room. Some of them tinkled too loudly and moved too much for the elf's liking—like nervous thoughts about to break through to a conscious mind.

"We'd better remain to the sides of the room to avoid any falling objects," he cautioned.

A little farther down the room, a tall arch led into a long corridor. From there they could see a broad staircase that wound up into the darkness. As they entered the corridor, they saw that it was yet another catacomb bedecked with bones in a garish display like the tunnels below.

"The catacombs reach all the way up here?" the elf asked no one in particular. "Or do the nobles just like to fill their buildings with crypts and decorate all their hallways with human remains?"

"You didn't know?" Dame Logan asked.

"Know what?" the elf replied.

"Everyone who dies in Spiral is transported up to the Noble Tier. That's why it's called Heaven."

The elf gave Dame Logan a long look.

"I didn't understand it either," Dame Logan said. "Until now I thought the Nobles just confiscated what valuables they could find in the coffins and on the corpses, then fed them to the birds or pitched them over the edge of the mother-of-pearl. I assumed that all the talk about coming to Heaven for long and loyal service down below was just platitudes. But people do indeed die and go to Heaven."

The scientist grinned.

"No, they don't," the elf said. "They're made into construction material and decoration for the royal castle."

"Exactly," Dame Logan laughed.

"It's not funny," the elf said. "Well, just a little bit." When he thought about it he couldn't help but smile at the irony, too.

"Grandmother," Alexandra said and pulled at Dame Logan's sleeve. "Promise me we won't die here. I don't want to become wall decoration—even for a rich person."

Dame Logan smiled at her granddaughter. "I promise. We shan't die here, but somewhere far, far away where they don't use the dead as mold work."

After that there was just one way to go, and that was up to the light they had seen flickering farther above in the castle.

Nine
The Castle Corpse

It was a long and tedious journey in the darkness, up steep and rickety stairs and down endless bone-lined hallways. Occasionally, they passed rooms that were furnished but devoid of people. These ranged in size from enormous mirrored ballrooms like the one they had passed through earlier to tall throne rooms or long dinner halls with tables for more than a hundred people to modestly-sized drawing rooms and small dressing chambers. These rooms for the living, as the elf came to regard them, invariably sat on the wall that faced outward with windows to let in fresh air. The rooms on the opposite side, the charnel side, were yet more tombs and catacombs. They even passed a few large spaces that had what looked like headstones and marble needles dug into the floor as memorials for the dead.

At one point on their journey through the dead halls, they passed an open oak door. A faint gray illumination emitted from the room inside, the sleepy light of the hour just before dawn.

"A bedroom!" the elf said, enthusiastically. They usually contained beds, and that was exactly what he needed now. The muted morning light streamed in from windows, which were two stories tall and lined with heavy wine-red draperies tied together with stout golden tassels. A burgundy carpet with golden patterns swirling in the handwoven thread covered the floor. A massive bed in dark lacquered wood with feet shaped like a lion's and a canopy in yellow damask sat along the inner wall. The bed was made with a deep red comforter that had not a wrinkle in its surface.

They raced to the bed and threw themselves down on the thick cover with great sighs. But after a few minutes, when they were all nearly asleep, the elf forced himself up, shut the door, and pushed the low broad chairs that stood in the corner in front of the door and the pot-bellied commode in the other corner in front the chairs.

"Are you afraid that ghosts will disturb our sleep?" Dame Logan chuckled.

"With this many dead people around?" the elf muttered. "I certainly am."

The work done, the elf finally collapsed on the bed alongside his companions. The gray cat curled warmly up on his thighs. With the door shut and secured, they fell asleep on the bed with the comforter over them and slept well into the day.

THE ELF LIFTED his head and squinted into the room. No ghosts. Only a gray midday light of overcast weather. Oh, it had been such a long time since he had slept in a good bed like this and rested his back and hips properly. It had been—despite him getting an elbow in the side from either Dame Logan or Alexandra, and the cat lying on his legs so the muscles became stiff and sore—the most comfortable night in a long time.

When the others began to stir as well the elf got up. By the far window stood a small wooden cabinet with a hole in the top. The elf opened its beautifully carved doors and found a tall pitcher with an elegantly curving handle and beautiful pattern of gilt leaves on one side sitting in a white porcelain bowl with a golden rim.

The pitcher was almost full of clear water. It looked clean. The elf sniffed it. It didn't smell rotten and only had a little dust on its surface. The elf took a small sip. The water tasted good, although it was still and had been standing there a while. He shared it with Alexandra, Dame Logan, and the cat, and they enthusiastically drained the pitcher.

Thirst quenched, the elf spotted a large silver bowl on a desk by the window, containing several small red apples. They were wrinkled and soft but had not yet decayed into blackness. The elf distributed them evenly, and they ate the mealy fruits as if they were the best meal they ever had.

The desk had a sloping lid with a curling pattern of inlaid dark wood and mother-of-pearl. Curious, the elf opened the desk and found several tiny shelves inside stacked with yellowed stationery paper, ink, blotter, seal, wax, and a small stamp. The elf tried the stamp on a sheet of paper and grinned when the letters on the crest announced it as the seal of the royal family of Spiral. Using his finest, most unintelligible hand and noblest, most eloquent words, the elf scratched a brief letter of introduction, presenting himself and his companions "to whomever it may concern," stamped, and sealed it with the coat of arms of whomever had lived in the burgundy bedroom. He then stuffed the stamp, seal, wax, and some sheets of stationery into the hidden pockets of his robes.

Adjacent to the bedroom was a small bathroom with white walls, alternating black and white tiles on the floor, a curved porcelain tub, and a toilet of the same dark wood as the cabinet in the bedroom. The stench from the hole in the toilet was almost overpoweringly strong, but they were all nevertheless very relieved for the opportunity to use it. They even found a couple of brass candle holders and candlesticks in the room.

"I'll take those," Dame Logan told the elf. "You wave your arms around too much and have long sleeves. That's a fire hazard."

Then it was time to continue farther up into the building. They stayed in the outer corridor to be able to see some inhabited rooms from time to time and to stay as far away from the burial chambers as possible. Thus, they traversed the outer side of the castle-corpse just beneath its cold surface but saw no one and met no one.

ANOTHER DAY OF gray light and seemingly endless travel ensued. They trudged in silence, lit by Dame Logan's white candles. Twice they stopped to eat more of the mealy overripe apples they had found in the bedroom. It wasn't much, but it was better than nothing. Even here, the charnel corridor went on for long stretches where it seemed to be devoid of rooms for the living.

"What was that?" Alexandra suddenly whispered. "I thought I heard something."

"It's a ghost," the elf hissed.

"No, it's not. Don't be stupid," Dame Logan said while she waved the candleholder around.

"Then why are you doing that with the light?" the elf said.

"Shh," Alexandra said. "It's voices."

They all fell quiet and listened intently. Unfortunately for the elf, it was no ghost. The sound came from an open doorway farther down the corridor. They were hearing human voices, the tail end of a serious conversation, which was taking place in the distant room.

"Who's going to bring the king his food?" asked a huffing male voice. "It's already done, and it must be served before it gets cold. Where are those damn Vertigis when you need them?"

"As I just told you, Freelord Montgomery," a sharp voice shot back, "the Vertigis are sick. That is to say, those of them who are not dead already. The same with your family—and mine. You are now the only Montgomery who's not bedridden."

The person who said this was clearly female and spoke in a high-pitched nasal tone.

"Sod those lazy bastards," the man replied. There was a low bang, maybe from Freelord Montgomery kicking furniture. "Nascence," he continued, "I hope for your sake you have some replacement waiters!"

"How can you worry about that now?" the female voice asked. "People are dying, and the only thing you care about is whether the king gets his meal on time or not?"

There was another bang.

"Shut your impudent mouth, Nascence," the lord said. "You know very well that if the king does not get his meals on time, the king's consort will flog me for failing my duties."

"Last I saw the king's consort, she was fainted in her own sick, so she probably has other matters to attend to than your well-earned punishment," Freelady Nascence replied, then walked off, her shoes clacking against the floor.

From the hallway the enticing smell of simmering food and the sound of running water reached the travelers, and their stomachs knotted in hunger.

"This is perfect!" the elf whispered. "If the king is sick, we can more easily persuade him to add Dame Logan's discovery to the official teachings."

"Do you ever think about anyone but yourself?!" Dame Logan hissed.

The elf looked at her, incredulous. "I just did. I was thinking about you and your grand theorem."

"Look," Dame Logan said. "If the king and the nobles are sick, we need to help them."

"But it's no wonder they are sick," the elf said. "They live in a tomb."

"I think there must be something more to it than that," Dame Logan said. "Don't forget all the inhabited rooms we passed. They only seemed as if they had been empty for a few days."

"All right," the elf said. "Let's offer our culinary services to the royals and see what is going on."

"Can't we just say that we're physicians who have come to help them?" Alexandra asked.

"That's a brilliant idea, my girl," Dame Logan said, smiling.

"No!" the elf said. "That means we will have to get close to diseased people and clean up their sick and maybe even worse things. And what happens when they discover we're not making anyone better? Unless one of you actually did study medicine."

Alexandra shook her head. Dame Logan, too.

"Does anyone know how to cook then?" Alexandra said. "I don't."

"Didn't you hear what they were saying?" the elf whispered. "The food has already been made. They just need someone to serve it to the king. Easy access and all that."

Dame Logan nodded. "Noble cooks it is then."

"But I implore you," the elf said. "Protect yourselves against the miasma!" He took out his least favorite scarf, ripped it in two, and handed one part to Dame Logan and the other to Alexandra. He then pulled his own silken scarf up over his nose and mouth. "Always have this in front of your nose and mouth, don't touch your faces, and never lick your hands!"

Dame Logan and Alexandra tied the cloth in front of their faces while the cat nuzzled the elf's lapels and vanished inside his robes.

In the flickering light from Dame Logan's candle, the elf produced a new missive with the noble stationery and seal. It presented them as distant members of the Vertigis family—royal waiters and sommeliers who had just returned to Spiral after some time abroad. The elf hoped the Vertigis would be so far down the royal hierarchy that members of the family actually did travel abroad. This done, they hurried to the doorway of the next room.

FOR BEING THE royal kitchen, and compared with gargantuan rooms they had seen elsewhere in the castle-corpse, the kitchen was surprisingly small. It was paved with yellow flagstones, which crunched with sand, dust, dried peels, and crumbs. The walls were a sun-kissed yellow blotched with moisture and ended in a wide chimney that pierced the low greasy ceiling. The main work station was a long counter that ran beneath the small windows. The counter was covered with glazed white tiles to enable a smooth work surface and easy cleaning. It glistened in the flickering light from the oil lamps in the ceiling. On the tiles lay half a slaughtered cow, thick bundles of green leeks, onions, garlic, mushrooms, green and white asparagus, radishes, potatoes, bottles of golden oil and vinegar, syrup, honey, wines, mounds of peppercorns, salt crystals, rare white sugar, brown sugar, loaves of long bread, round bread, flat bread, black truffle, ground meat, sausages, dried ham, cured ham, fresh fish, dried fish, salted fish, scallops, and plates of black chocolate, brown chocolate, and white chocolate. In short the best and finest produce Spiral and its tributary villages and farmsteads could offer.

Nevertheless, all of the food had clearly been there for days. Some was rotten already, and everything else would need to be boiled, fried, baked, or heavily seasoned before it could be eaten. In the corner behind the door, a wide copper cabinet stood open, stacked almost full with wood logs.

From a long spout beneath the windows, clear water trickled down into a broad garbage-filled sink. Next to it, the tile-covered counter ended in a large stove with eight rings for cooking. Here black iron pots and pans stood full of simmering dishes. When the scientist and the girl and the cat and the elf saw that, they almost ran into each other to help themselves to the food.

ONLY THE STERN voice of Freelord Montgomery stopped them. A short broad-shouldered man with a round belly, bald head, and a thick black moustache that reached all the way to the angles of his broad lower jaw stood leaning against the worktop. He was dressed in a white jacket with a golden bandelier across the chest, golden tasseled epaulets, and a gold chain reaching from his red vest to the outer pocket. Below his waist his body tapered into two thin legs in a pair of pantaloons that had once been white and a pair of black riding boots. The elf thought the Freelord managed to look ridiculous and dignified at the same time. The rotund noble was mopping his face and neck with a dirty handkerchief.

When he saw them enter the room he jumped up and shouted:

"Halt! Who goes there?"

His voice reverberated against the dirty white tiles. Beneath his broad black eyebrows the Freelord's eyes were squinty and blue. Currently, his face looked feverishly pale.

The elf made his most flourishing and impressive bow and motioned for the others to do the same. "My name is Elv of Vertigi. I have been ordered here to help out in the serving of our esteemed royals," the elf announced and presented the fake letter of introduction with both hands to the Freelord.

On seeing this the Freelord looked both relieved and suspicious at the same time. He picked up the letter from the elf's hands and rolled it open. A few drops of sweat fell down on the yellow paper as he read. Freelord Montgomery was one of those people who flickers their eyes and mouths the words while reading. Beneath his scarf the elf grinned broadly and had to work to not let his smile reach his eyes.

"Very well," said the Freelord when he was finally done. "I shall check your lineages more closely in the morning to evaluate if you are of properly noble birth to serve a king his food, but for now you are accepted. Due to the acute absenteeism we are currently having, I doubt anyone will think twice of letting you serve."

"Thank you so much, Master of the Royal Kitchen," the elf said and bowed again, this time with fewer flourishes to finish more quickly.

"Freelord Montgomery will do very well, thank you," the noble said.

Once again the elf only managed to stop his snicker just in time. "Please excuse our masks," the elf continued. "Our physician claims it may help stop spreading the disease."

"Really?" asked the Freelord with raised eyebrows. "I shall take note of that and take up the habit. We should be doing everything in our power to halt this terrible contagion. I'm sure you know it has taken a terrible toll on us."

"Indeed," the elf said, lowering his eyes. "We are nevertheless ready to work and strongly motivated to prepare and serve the meals for the king."

"Splendid! Splendid!" Freelord Montgomery said and smoothed down his big moustache. "When you have plated the food talk with the good Freelady Nascence in the anteroom next door. She will instruct you further. All menus are listed on the wall. You will find the next meal to be readied there."

The elf bowed again like an obedient noble servant.

"Please excuse me," the burly man said and hurried toward the door. "I have some important matter to attend to right away."

The elf bowed again.

"NOW WHAT?" THE elf thought as he turned toward the stove where eight large black pots were bubbling and frothing. Dame Logan was already at the wall reading. Above the worktop thin panels of black wood had been mounted. On them the ingredients for and instructions on how to prepare the royal meals had been written in golden longhand. The script slanted steeply to the right and contained many thin loops and flurries. To the elf it looked more like ribbons than writing.

"Can you read these panels?" the elf asked Dame Logan.

"Of course," Dame Logan replied. "And it seems that today's main meal has already been made. But we have to start on the evening meal right away."

"Could you and Alexandra do that while I bring the main meal to the king? I can't read the panels at all."

"All right," Dame Logan said. "But you'd better hurry back. There's a lot of food that needs to be prepared."

The elf nodded. "Do the panels say what I should bring the king first?"

"The panels don't mention a sequence," Dame Logan said and tilted her head at the cauldrons on the stoves. "Only that everything must be served and in their cauldrons."

"Everything?" the elf said. "That's a lot of food." He had hoped some of it was meant for other nobles or the staff.

"Seems so," Dame Logan said. "Maybe the whole cauldrons are brought in to ensure the food is hot when it finally arrives in the royal chamber."

The elf took a pair of thick mitts that hung from a copper bar on the stove, pulled them on, and took hold of the first enormous pot. It contained food for at least ten people, a thick orange bubbling stew. The cauldron was so heavy the elf barely managed to lift it. Behind him he heard Dame Logan start to recite for Alexandra the ingredients they needed to prepare the next meal.

"Onions, butter, garlic, side of beef ..."

THE ELF HAD to drag the pot along the floor to the end of the kitchen. The door was reinforced by a metal plate at the bottom and the side where one would normally find a handle. But there was no handle. Instead, the door had large hinges that allowed it to swing both inward and outward. Panting, the elf leaned into the door, pushed against it, and pulled the cauldron after him. Small puddles of orange stew were left after him on the sandy floor.

Beyond the swinging kitchen door a lean woman in a tight-fitting high-necked black dress with a black hairdo that stretched toward the heavens rose from a narrow chair at the opposite door. The chair was made of the same dark elegantly carved wood as they had seen in the empty bedroom and elsewhere in the castle, and the seat and back held an embroidered pattern of a bouquet of roses in pale hues of purple, yellow, orange, pink, and white. Next to the chair was a table in the same dark wood and another chair with a similar embroidered pattern.

The elf bowed as best as he could while supporting the large pot on the floor. "Lord Vertigi to serve the king his main meal for the day," he said.

The tall woman adjusted the round spectacles on the tip of her long nose. Her hands were covered with black lace gloves. "You are late," she said and looked down at him from the corner of her dark eyes. "Ladle soup into a bowl and serve it to the king. What he doesn't want you discard into the hole at the end of the room. Is that understood?"

"Yes."

"And you are under no circumstances allowed to speak to the king unless he addresses you first. Then you lower your gaze and reply as quickly and as accurately as you can. The king's time is invaluable. Do you understand?"

"Yes," said the elf and bowed again. But inside he was laughing. Now he knew what rules to break and how to cause the most annoyance.

Finally, the woman in black let him pass through the opposite door and sat down in the embroidered chair, wiping her forehead and the sides of her nose. She too was looking a little feverish, the elf noticed. Were they all sick?

The elf pushed against the white-and-golden double door and drew a deep breath. Finally, he'd get to see the king. Now he just had to make his appeal strong and valid for the monarch so that he could persuade the ruler to let Dame Logan's theorem into the official records of the city. Or at the very least, let Dame Logan present her theorem for the king.

***

He stood in another of the castle-corpse's gargantuan rooms. This was the enormous building at the top of the heap which they had seen from the first window they found. It was only afternoon, but since it was late fall the sun was already about to set. Only a weak moon lit the blue darkness outside.

In here the floor was as dirty as the kitchen had been. Sand, dust, and gravel crunched beneath the elf's narrow shoes, and several of the columns that flanked the aisle he was progressing down had toppled to the floor. Above him impossibly tall, thin stone arches held up a deeply vaulted ceiling. The stone masonry was so high and narrow it seemed to defy gravity itself. Dame Logan should see this, the elf thought. The arches looked like mathematics in motion.

But like the floor, the walls and windows were dirty and worn. Streams of rainwater had followed the columns from the ceiling to the floor and left dark weep marks on the white stone. He could hear water dripping from farther inside the vaulted space. Along the aisle was a track of whiter stone, a path created by the earlier servants in the grime. When they had first spotted the room the distance and moonlight had entirely beautified the old structure. While it was taller and more beautiful and spacious than any other place in the castle-corpse, or any other building he had seen for that matter, no architectural magic or sheen of extreme status could hide the ruin that dominated the place. Even here the charnel stench hung heavy in the air, and the temperature was more like the morgue than anywhere else.

As the elf approached the end, he had to pull the large pot up five stairs while clanging the feet of the pot into the dirty marble, spilling tomato and beef stew on the stairs, adding to the decades of food that had been left there. His arms and back were aching so much he had to take a break to stretch for every step, slowing his advance even further.

Even nearer the end of the enormous space there was a little more light. Here several tables and chests stood covered with hundreds of white and golden wax candles. These filled the surfaces of furniture, even sat directly on the floor, and had spilled onto and melted into each other. Burned candles hadn't been replaced or removed; more candles had simply been placed over them. The mounds of white wax still held several flames and short charred wicks.

By the mounds of candles were an enormous white canopy bed withdrawn golden draperies. This bed was larger than the bedroom they had spent the night in on the way up to the monarch's kitchen. A small portable staircase in dark carved wood led up to one side of the bed. Past the candles an enormous hole gaped blackly in the floor. It was almost as large as the royal bed, easily the length of seven men across, and nearly completely circular. Sections of the rim had collapsed and fallen into the abyss. Other places along it seemed safe as countless feet had shuffled a trail in the candle wax and dust. Green mold, brown fungi, yellow lichen, and variously colored remains of food hung off the edge of the hole. It looked like the maw of a terrible, always hungry monster.

Now the elf knew where the king's leftovers were to be discarded. Slowly, painfully, the elf dragged the pot over to the portable stairs at the side of the royal bed. Here tall stacks of white porcelain plates and a mound of silver spoons had been left on the floor. For some reason all the plates were bowls. Did the king eat only soups and stews? Perhaps he was so old he no longer had any teeth to chew with?

THE ELF RESTED the cauldron on the floor. He was glad he didn't have to carry its full contents back to the kitchen, yet the prospect of discarding almost all of the food, easily a meal for ten, down the huge hole was sickening. He wasn't going to do that unless he had eaten a little of it himself. He was so hungry, and who would see him here? The king sat behind the curtains on the giant canopy bed. The elf picked a bowl from the top of the nearest stack on the floor and chose a spoon from the mound of tableware next to it. It was all covered with black oxidation.

The stew was still warm and steaming and smelled wonderfully as the elf ladled it into the dusty bowl. Then he climbed the portable stairs to the enormous bed and announced the meal as served. His voice reverberated into the semi-darkness. There was no reply. The elf announced the meal once more. He waited a long moment in silence while he wondered what was worse: disturbing the king in his sleep or bringing him a cold meal. Finally, the elf pulled the drapes aside, climbed up on the vast, undulating mattress, and began to approach the figure that was sitting in the middle of the bed propped up by the white and gold headboard.

Ten
The Discovery

As the elf approached the monarch, he realized that something was terribly wrong. The king slumped against a multitude of white and golden tasseled pillows in a rather twisted and rather uncomfortable-looking position. There was almost no hair left on his head, only a few long strands that stuck out between a band of corroded gold. The king's eyes were huge and black and in shadow. His body was extremely emaciated with just tatters of flesh and white ermine fur hanging off the bones. The king was dead and had been so for a long time.

When the elf saw that, he screamed, dropped the plate, and bounded off the mattress in long, wobbly jumps. On the way out of the drapes, he almost fell into the enormous hole that gaped on that side of the bed.

"Ahh!" the elf shouted and somehow managed to twist around so that he landed at the edge of the hole. Several floor tiles shook loose and fell into the darkness. Prone and wide-eyed, the elf still had the presence of mind to listen for the clatter when the tiles finally hit the bottom.

There was none.

There was only silence.

"Ahh!" thought the elf when he realized he would not have survived the fall. Slowly and carefully, so as not to break off more of the floor, he crawled away from the unstable rim. Then the smell hit him.

The constant draft from the windows on the outer wall must have ceased for a while or the direction of the air momentarily shifted, revealing the nauseating stench that rose from the hole. When it reached the elf's nose his eyes filled with tears and his throat closed up. He had to gasp for air. He had thought the smell of the catacombs and the putrid food in the kitchen was the worst assault his sense of smell would ever experience, but this was worse—much, much worse. It was also dangerous since it smelled so badly it seemed to be able to rob him of his breath. As quickly as he could manage, the elf got to his feet and stumbled away from the hole, hoping there was not a similar abyss on the other side of the room hiding in the darkness.

There wasn't a hole but a large wooden barrel. The elf banged into it but managed to throw his arms up to protect his head just in time. Once more he fell to the dirty floor and rolled around in pain for a while. When he finally could see again he touched his forehead, and his fingers came away red. A closer examination showed that he had a small cut on the side of his forehead, but like all head wounds, it bled profusely. The elf fished out a handkerchief from somewhere in the robes and pressed it against his skin. Then he looked up.

In the light from the mound of candles by the king's bed, a small hill of barrels, boxes, chests, caches, bags, satchels, and sacks rose in front of him. From these came spilled fabrics, leathers, seeds, flowers, tools, masonry, paintings, mosaics, fireworks, stained glass windows, stationery, shields, swords, bows, spears, armors, even a whole ballista, dresses, robes, hats, shoes, boots, books, scrolls, writing implements, rugs, pillows, tables, chairs, shelves, lamps, sofas—everything the mind could ever desire or think of as desirable, whether it was necessary or useful or not. Even the dried husks of a few animal corpses lay in the heap: a cow, a sheep, a pig, a turkey, and even a horse.

THE ELF STOOD, blinking. He swallowed and tried to take in the entire mound and the thousands of different items that lay stacked inside the royal bedchamber. What was all this? The remains of the enormous pile of tributes sent from the lower strata of Spiral to the Noble Tier every day? It had to be. The items could not have come from anywhere else. This was where all the livestock and food and weapons and tools and other objects transported up through the gates every day ended up. In a stinking, empty hell.

For a while the elf felt paralyzed by the sight of all the wasted goods, as well as the realization that the time, effort, and energy that had gone into fashioning all those items had been wasted. It was a daunting, saddening, and shocking revelation.

And why had the objects been abandoned here instead of being used by the nobles who must have been aware that the king had been dead for a long time. Why hadn't they put all the items to good use? No one in the lower tiers would have been the wiser. Then it hit the elf, even harder than the previous insights. These items had not been used because there were no one to use them. The population in the noble tier could not be large, and as the conversation between Freelord Montgomery and Freelady Nascence had indicated, it must be have been dwindling.

***

WHEN THOUGHTS BECAME too busy or too loud the elf felt it was best to sit down and ignore them for a while to let the body catch up to them. He sat down by the wide barrel he had run into, leaned back, and relaxed. He stretched his legs out so the pointed toes of his shoes peeked out beneath the hem of his once-fine robe. There the elf hummed a small song for himself and drew spirals in the dust on the dirty bedchamber floor.

What did it all mean? Who could he ask to confirm that it meant what he thought it meant? And what, if anything, should he do about it? He looked from the corpse in the bed to the black maw on the floor to the mound of unused goods that towered above it. The items were too decrepit to be returned to the citizens of Spiral. And the King was long since dead. That much was clear.

"Elf! Elf!"

The shout echoed through the royal bedchamber, thrown about and reflected by all the hard surfaces. The elf turned and squinted down the semi-darkness to the door. Far down there a small figure was waving her arms while at the same time propping the door open with one foot. It was Alexandra.

"Elf!" she shouted. "Where are you?"

"Here!" the elf shouted and waved at the girl. Alexandra looked up and waved when she spotted him. She looked around, let go of the door, and began to move out into the dark chamber.

"No! the elf shouted. "Stay there! I'm done! Go back to the kitchen!" He did not want Alexandra to experience the ugly sight and the deathly smell at the end of the royal bedchamber. He got to his feet and ran down the aisle of the cold, dead room. From the open door, light and warmth leaked out from the antechamber, bringing with it the smell of food. At the scent of the stew, the elf's stomach constricted and made an audible growl. Well, it was not like the king needed the food anymore. The elf, however, definitely needed some sustenance after the horrible shock and the killing smell. He pulled the door open and stepped into the light and the noise and life of the kitchen.

"I hope the food ...!" he began, but cut himself short when he accidentally kicked something soft on the floor. A heap of black, dusty fabric and black hair loosened from a very tall bun lay on the floor. Freelady Nascence's face still looked pale and sweaty. Even her dark eyes had taken on a white sheen in death.

Was it she who had kept the secret of the dead king all these years, the elf wondered. It couldn't be. Freelady Nascence did not serve the king his meals. That had been the task of the Vertigi family. The good Freelady had only let the noble waiters and waitresses into the royal bedchamber and maybe announced their presence on the way. Thus, more people must have known about the king.

"What happened to her?" the elf asked.

"I don't know," Alexandra said behind her piece of the elf's former scarf. "I found her like this. I think she's dead."

The elf nodded. "Yes, she is," he said. "It must be the illness they talked about. Keep your scarf on and don't touch her. Did you touch her?"

"No," Alexandra said. "I just pushed her over with my foot to see who it was."

"Good," the elf said. "Let's not touch her. She may still be full of miasma."

"I guess we know where she's going now," Alexandra said laconically, but her face was full of regret.

The elf gave a little laugh. "Yes, for Spiral's nobility the distance from the cradle to the grave is not very far."

THEY RETURNED TO the kitchen. Now the long, low room was filled with mist. Dame Logan was cooking so hard that condensation ran down the windows and covered the walls and ceiling like sweat. On the stove seven black cauldrons and an enormous frying pan were going at full boil. The pan was wider than three normal-sized pans put together and filled with a ham and potato omelette sprinkled generously with some kind of red powdered spice and garnished with green pieces of spring onion. The elf could see the yellow mass hid sliced tomatoes and bits of fried bacon. Dame Logan had left a long wooden ladle in the pan to stir the omelette with. It smelled of all the various ingredients that were in it, both sweet and aromatic and salty and slightly off due to the stale eggs and meat. To the elf it smelled sweeter than heaven.

On the bench next to the enormous frying pan sat a pitcher of water drawn from the ever-running faucet. The beads that sat on the white porcelain told the elf that the water inside was still cold. He grabbed the pitcher and drank from it so the water flowed over the corners of his mouth and dribbled down his chin. Still he kept drinking, long deep draughts that threatened to come out his nose. When he was done he set the pitcher down, wiped his face with the back of his hand, and plunged the long ladle into the golden omelette and ate it straight from the pan.

"What the hell do you think you're doing?!" Dame Logan yelled. She had found a white, relatively clean apron in the cupboard under the sink along with a tall white hat that was made of such thin, stiff fabric that it stood erect by itself. The hat reached more than three feet into the air, but she wore it because its headband would keep sweat out of her eyes and prevent stray hairs from her loose bun from falling into the food.

Had the circumstances been less hunger-filled, the elf would have laughed loudly at the odd outfit, but now he could do nothing but chew and swallow and bite into the soft mixture of egg, potato, bacon, onion, and tomato that filled his mouth. "We can eat everything we want!" he shouted between chewing. "Everything we want!"

Dame Logan's eyes lit up.

Had she really not eaten any of the ingredients or the food she had been preparing, wondered the elf. The woman was either insane or extremely dedicated. Then he remembered Logan's theorem. Of course she wouldn't want any chances of offending the monarch. He was, after all, the person who was going to reinstate Dame Logan and declare her theorem as official truth.

"Did the king say we could eat as much as we want?" Dame Logan yelled.

It was the first time the elf had heard the scientist raise her voice above the volume of normal conversation. He kept chewing and swallowing the food. It was the best meal he had had. It felt like he was eating his way back to life and away from the brink of that horrible bottomless pit that lay sleeping inside the darkness of the royal bedchamber.

When Dame Logan saw the elf's nods she ran over to the cauldrons that stood bubbling on the stove. Then she dug the ladle into one of the simmering dishes and filled her mouth with it. She did not need to ask Alexandra twice to join in on their feast.

STRANGELY, OR FORTUNATELY, depending on which way you look at it, hunger has the peculiar characteristic that it is painful when it is there and also painful when it is not there. That is to say, both when the body is very hungry and also when it is very full. That was what the scientist and the girl and the elf now experienced.

The elf leaned into the stove behind him while he clutched his stomach and slid down on the floor. On the way to a more horizontal position, he saw that the huge pan whose omelette he had just devoured was now only two-thirds full. He had eaten a portion of food fit more for two people than one. "Oh, dear gods," he groaned and cursed his eyes for being hungrier than his belly. He laid down on the sandy floor, but that only made his stomach ache more, so he sat up and leaned into the warm stove.

Next to him, Dame Logan and Alexandra did the same. Dame Logan had single-handedly lowered the level of beef and butter stew in the vat-like pot while Alexandra had sampled a little of everything. They had served the little gray cat some stew directly on the floor along with a puddle of fresh water. Now even the cat had a visible bulge on her belly and lay sideways on the aprons and kitchen towels inside the shelf under the work top.

"I must say," Dame Logan groaned. "How very gracious of the king to share his meal with us."

The elf was on the brink of sleep and only heard Dame Logan mention the king. "Well, of course he did," the elf muttered, half in dreams. "Seeing he's deceased and has no use for the food."

Dame Logan sat up. The elf could almost hear her think "What?" before she said it.

"Oh," said the elf and burped. "I wasn't going to tell you that until later."

"Dear sweet gods!" the scientist groaned. "Did you kill the king so that he couldn't refuse my theorem?"

Now it was the elf's turn to sit up. "No! Certainly not! Who do you think I am?" But now Dame Logan was crying. "What's wrong now then?"

"What's wrong now?" Dame Logan echoed in a shrill tone. "I'll tell you what's wrong! If the king is dead, no matter if you killed him or not, he cannot sign the official reinstatement papers! And my theorem will never gain the recognition it should!"

The scientist broke down in tears again. Her memory of the very large and pleasant meal seemed to be forgotten already.

The elf groaned. Couldn't he get a moment's peace? "Ah yes, I suppose that is a little issue now," he said. He did have another follow-up thought to that, but it faded from his mind as he searched for something comforting to say. His eyes closed. He was about to fall asleep. Dame Logan must have been tired, too, because after that the elf didn't hear anything more for a long while.

***

WHEN HE WOKE it was dark outside and the oil in the kitchen lamps was almost out. The little flames were flickering madly, casting long, thin shadows on the walls. The fire in the stoves had gone out, too, but when the elf opened the metal lid behind him the embers were still red. Food and sleep had revitalized him greatly. Now he felt almost like he had before all the running and climbing and arguing. Dame Logan and the girl lay still sprawled on the floor. The cat was sleeping on her spot inside the cupboard. The elf got up, found the largest remaining pot he could, one that was almost half his height, lugged it over to the running tap, rinsed it a few times, and filled it with water. He could barely lift it but pushed it along the bench to the nearest plate on the stove. Then he took the lid, emptied one of the ladles, and banged the steel cover a few times.

"Wake up, wake up! Time to go to work!" the elf yelled.

"Wha—huh?" Dame Logan said in midsnore, then groaned when she realized she was being awakened. Alexandra opened her eyes and glared at them both. The cat did the same but decided to ignore them and curled back up into a ball.

"Good evening, friends, colleagues, and travel companions," the elf said formally. "In my rejuvenating sleep I have had the opportunity to reflect on our current difficult situation. And I have decided that we will approach it in a calm and rational manner." He looked at the companions. The words sounded pretty good in his ears. But Dame Logan looked less than impressed.

"Of course we shall approach it in a calm and rational manner," the scientist said. "Because that is the only way to approach anything."

Alexandra simply yawned and stretched.

"Yes, and I have a plan," said the elf. "Thanks to you and the girl."

"Oh, gods," Dame Logan groaned.

***

THE ELF INSTRUCTED Alexandra to refill the lamps with oil from the cupboard, then heat the water in the large pot to a boil, and let it bubble until the level of water sank. In the meantime the elf wanted to show Dame Logan the king and the royal bedchamber.

"Steel yourself for a bad sight and an even worse smell," he told the scientist when he opened the door to the antechamber. When Dame Logan saw the good servant Freelady Nascence dead on the floor she gasped.

"Is she ...?"

"Yes," the elf said. "Come on, grab her feet. We need to get her out before she starts smelling up the kitchen."

Behind her scarf Dame Logan's eyes went narrow. "This is a most terrible disease. How do we know we won't catch it?"

"We don't know," said the elf. "But I have one measure we can try. It's the best I can do." He expected Dame Logan to start protesting, but the scientist didn't say anything more and hunched to take hold of Lady Nascence's black-stockinged ankles. Even the soles of her narrow-heeled lace boots were all black.

They carried the dead noble into the enormous bedchamber and up the aisle. They had to rest several times before they reached the stairs that led up to the area with the bed.

Dame Logan looked around, her eyes wide and dark. "Is this the king's bedroom?" she asked.

The elf nodded.

"And this is the building we saw on the top of the castle-mound?"

The elf nodded again.

"But there's no one here."

"It gets worse," the elf said.

WHEN DAME LOGAN saw the skeletal king in the giant bed and the hill of unused and rotting tributes and smelled the stench from the black hole she ran behind the royal bed and lost what was left of her dinner. While the scientist was busy being sick, the elf carried the dead servant noble as close to the hole as he dared, then gave the body a good kick so it rolled to the edge and fell into the darkness without a sound. Again the elf listened for the sound of landing, but again there was none— just a long, eerie silence and the sound of the draft whistling through the room.

"This ... this is terrible!" Dame Logan said when he returned from behind the bed, wiping her lips with the back of her hand. "And nothing short of pathological."

The elf nodded. "No wonder the lower tiers, even the noble families, are barred from visiting the royals," he said. "What do you think would happen if this got out?"

"This?" Dame Logan said. "That the king is dead, or that he is—or rather was—insane?"

"Both," grinned the elf. It was good to share the secret with someone else even if it was a terrible secret.

"Well," Dame Logan considered. "The king is after all dead, so we do not need to tell anyone that he was insane. If there are any heirs, I suppose they will be crowned as the new regent. Or the next in line among the nobles will."

"That's it!" the elf said, even happier than before. He knew it had been smart to discuss these things with the scientist. "Let's go and find an heir, and then she can adjudicate your theorem."

Dame Logan looked at him. "But wait! If we tell anyone, they will know that we non-nobles have been inside the king's bedchamber. They might not like that very much."

"Hmm," the elf said. "We could show them that we have a letter of presentation."

"The more people who see it, the higher the chance will be that we run into an actual member of the Vertigi family, and they will know that we are not one of them."

"That is true."

The elf thought. He stood pondering with his chin in his hand for a good while. Suddenly he realized that Dame Logan had gone closer to the hole and was staring intently at it. "Be careful," the elf said. "The rim's unstable, and I've only tried one side. The other might not be completely safe either."

"This place is a madhouse!" Dame Logan said. "What do you think made this abyss?"

"I have no idea," the elf said. "But don't draw your breath too deeply there. The hole reeks even worse than the catacombs."

Dame Logan peered at the slanting rim and down into the darkness. "This reminds me of something I read about ages ago," she said after a while. "I think I know what this is."

"Really?" the elf said. "What is it?"

"How did the theory go?" the scientist said, recalling. "Oh, yes. Pits like these open up in the ground when pockets of water or gases leave, so that brittle, unstable minerals are left. If there is then a small stress, like a minor earthquake or the lightning strikes nearby, the whole pocket collapses and the stone and earth above it. If this pocket is near the surface, a deep hole called a sink hole is created there."

The elf smiled. "That sounds perfectly logical."

Dame Logan beamed, her nausea obviously forgotten. "Yes, doesn't it? This particular hole stinks of subterranean gases, so it may well have been formed by those gases."

"No wonder," said the elf. "With all the dead people rotting below."

"There you have it, my friend!" Dame Logan grinned, looking like a proud teacher. "That must be the source for the gases."

"Maybe I could make an apprentice some day?" the elf felt bold enough to ask.

"In a few years' time," Dame Logan said, and they laughed together.

THEY RETURNED TO the kitchen. Now the water in the largest pot had been boiled and cooled off. Alexandra helped the elf decant the boiled water into three deep bowls. Then all three of them washed their hands and faces and arms with baking soda and vinegar in the boiled water. The elf also cleaned the gray cat's paws and face and ears, much to her protest.

"Now let's see if we can find an heir to the king," the elf said.

"Hang on a little," Dame Logan said. "I have been thinking about that. What if all the nobles actually know that the king is dead?"

The elf wanted to dismiss that idea, but he knew Dame Logan's insights were worth listening to. "Do you really think so?" the elf said.

"I do," Dame Logan said. "Especially since he's been sitting in there for a while."

"That can't have been Freelady Nascence and Freelord Montgomery's dirty secret through the years?"

"In the beginning it probably was, but with different servants coming and going and many people working in the kitchen, nothing like that would remain secret for long."

The elf nodded. He could see the sense in Dame Logan's assumptions. "But if the king is dead, wouldn't some of them have been very eager to try to take the throne for themselves?" he asked.

Now it was Dame Logan's turn to nod. "You'd think that, and it fits everything I know about the Noble Tier, constant scheming and jockeying for power all the time, even worse than in Academia."

The elf laughed. "So why haven't they?"

"Could have been power games gone mad," Dame Logan said. "By the time someone came out on top to claim the throne, it was too late to announce the king's death without raising the suspicion of the Judges and Scholars. Or maybe the king's death was the final result of someone's power game, and they didn't want it to come out. It was easier to rule under the cover of a dead king. Who knows? I've never understood exactly how the minds in the Noble tier work, although there have been some interesting studies."

The elf nodded again. "So who's been giving the orders all this time?"

"That's a good question," the scientist said. "Could have been Freelady Nascence that was the king's 'mouth' all this time. Or the Vertigis."

SUDDENLY THEY HEARD loud noises from the hallway outside. Someone was coming, and there was a lot of them. The kitchen door flew open, and the tall Royal Guard from the Academy of Natural Sciences and his band of brothers burst through the door.

Instantly, the elf made himself look like the noble servant Freelady Nascence and Dame Logan into Freelord Montgomery. He hoped the transformation had been fast enough for the Guardians to not notice and that Dame Logan would be quick on the ball to play the game.

"Get out and wipe the dust off your boots before you enter the kitchen!" the elf yelled in the shrill voice of Freelady Nascence. "Royal food is being cooked here!"

The tall Royal Guardian stood a moment, then huffed, and retreated back into the hallway. There he started kicking the dust off his boots while his five compatriots did the same.

"Play along," the elf whispered to Dame Logan, who was looking quite surprised but still had the presence of mind not to say anything. "You're Freelord Montgomery now."

"What?" Dame Logan said and looked down at herself. The elf wasn't certain the moustache and belly were big enough, and he may have missed some of the medals and decorations on the large man's chest; but he hoped no one would notice. Besides, nobles changed their medals, didn't they? Like jewelry? No one wore the same jewelry two days in a row?

It didn't last long till the Royal Guard was back. The elf pushed some brown hair out of his eyes. He hoped he was standing like a lady. "Thank you, guardsman," he said in the unfamiliar, high-pitched voice. "And what, pray tell, is the rush into the royal kitchens tonight? And quickly please. We have another meal to serve before the king is satisfied." It was probably best to let the Guardsman do the talking than forbid him outright to enter the kitchen.

The tall man bowed to the elf and then to Dame Logan, who was still looking a little flabbergasted but immediately started to stroke her big moustache.

"My apologies, honorable noble servant," the Guardsman said. "I have some terrible news, which the king must know of."

Interesting, thought the elf. "Is the news so terrible it needs to be brought to the king directly?" he said.

"It is, indeed," the Guardsman replied and bowed again.

Inwardly, the elf smiled. He could see why Freelady Nascence had kept the charade going. "Very well. I shall inquire the king if you may see him now. He is in the middle of his meal." To the elf's immense surprise his former captor bowed again.

The elf sashayed into the antechamber, closely followed by Freelord Montgomery, opened the kitchen door, then the door to the royal bedchamber. They heard the door to the kitchen swing shut.

"What do we do now?" Dame Logan asked in her Freelord Montgomery form. It was quite interesting to watch. It was Freelord Montgomery's shape and face and voice, but the inflection and the eyes were still Dame Logan's.

"I have a plan," said the elf.

THE FORM OF the noble servant Freelady Nascence brought some memories and explanations. She and Freelord Montgomery had simply pulled drapes of the Royal Bed shut so that the rare visitors could not see the king clearly. Then Freelord Montgomery had hid under the bed and used a brass loudspeaker to issue whatever royal orders had seemed appropriate at the time. The elf pulled Dame Logan farther into the royal bedchamber to avoid curious ears and explained everything to her quickly.

"You go over there, slide under the bed, and pretend to be the king," the elf said.

"But can't you just turn yourself into the king?" Dame Logan said.

"We don't know if the Guardsman is aware of the charade and just playing along for the sake of his fellows or if he truly knows nothing. Until we do, we just have to keep it up. Besides, I don't know what the king looked like alive, so I can't re-create his form."

"You turned me into a man," Dame Logan pouted.

The elf clicked his tongue. "It didn't hurt you and makes you able to speak for the king. I'll let the Guardsman in for his royal audience in five minutes."

Dame Logan looked in doubt, but before she had time to say anything more, the elf slipped through the antechamber door.

WHEN DAME LOGAN arrived at the bed she made sure the gold-on-white drapes were closed and hid between the wall and the bed. There she waited.

After a long, terrible wait she heard heavy but hesitant footsteps. The big Guardsman sounded like he was walking on eggshells, and his breath was ragged for having traversed the short distance from the kitchen to the king's bed. He was obviously very nervous. But as the Guard drew closer to the royal sleeping arrangement, his footfalls grew noticeably more determined and louder. Finally, the Guardsman stopped in front of the bed and bowed so deeply his leather belt and boots creaked.

"Speak and begone so I can finish my meal," Dame Logan demanded in Freelord Montgomery's deepest, most commanding voice.

The Guardsman looked around but then straightened his back and bowed again. "First Lord Guardsman of the Lower Noble Gate," he said, "the Judiciary Tier informs with the greatest reluctance and countless apologies that the dangerous criminal Scholar Logan and her companions, one adult male and one young female, escaped from prison in the storm three nights ago. We have reason to believe that the band of fugitives may be on their way here. Also," added the Guardsman, "a mysterious disease is taking its toll on the population of all tiers. The Scholars claim it was brought here with the storm."

When the Guardsman described the dangerous fugitives the scientist had to pinch herself to refrain from laughing. "How is the population faring?" she asked sternly instead. "And why didn't you mention that first? Without the populace, even in the lower tiers, we have no city."

The Guardsman shifted uneasily on his feet. "My deepest apologies, my King. I was merely worried about your safety, Your Majesty."

"Safety?" Dame Logan asked. "An old scholar and her friend and a girl. What harm should they do me, the king?"

"They have already blown up substantial parts of the Academy of Natural Sciences and ruined the prison of the Royal Judiciary Building."

"Do not be impertinent and talk back to your king!" Dame Logan commanded. "Besides, Royal Guardsman so and so, you are too late. I have already granted a pardon to the Scholar and her companions."

"What? But Your Majesty," protested the Guardsman. "These people are criminals! Enemies of the state!"

"Quiet," Dame Logan ordered. "The Scholar merely wanted to present her findings to me, and I allowed her. Furthermore, I concur with her findings. There will be a decree soon but bring the message to the Academy scribes that the Scholar Logan's findings are valid and will become official and right. Moreover, the Scholar's post at the Academy is fully reinstated. And see to it that her experimental model is repaired fully and delivered to her office at the Academy in due haste."

The information took a little while to sink into the mind of the Guardsman. Not the brightest of minds, the scientist concluded, but kept the silence royal.

"When it comes to the illness see to it that the populace is given enough water and food in these trying times," Dame Logan continued. "Divert resources from the Noble Gate if needed. Now leave. I am hungry."

"As you wish, Your Majesty," the Guardsman finally said, then started down the long path back to the kitchen.

WHEN THE ROYAL Guards had finally stomped out of the kitchen and Dame Logan told the elf what she had done the elf said:

"Are you certain this will work?"

"Of course, I'm sure," Dame Logan said. "And if not, you can fake a letter of pardon and a royal decree of my academic reinstatement."

The elf grinned and nodded. He took out the stationery he had left in the kitchen and began working on the important message. It took a while, but when he was done he blew on the ink and stamp to make them dry faster, folded the sheet together, stuffed it into an envelope and closed it with a seal. Then he gave the rest of the stationery, ink, and wax to the scholar.

Dame Logan looked at him, tears in her eyes. "How can I ever thank you for all of this?" she asked.

"You can't," the elf grinned. "But don't worry about it. Just return to your post at the Academy, spread your discovery to everyone, and stay out of trouble."

"Of course, I will," Dame Logan said and hugged the elf. The elf laughed and hugged her back.

"Can we go home now?" Alexandra asked.

Dame Logan nodded at her, beaming. "Are we all ready to leave?"

"Meow!" the cat said.

"I just need to do one thing first," the elf replied.

The elf ran down the aisle of the royal bedchamber, not worrying that his footfalls on the dusty floor echoed through the cold, dark room. It was time to quit this sad place of death and dust. Dame Logan, Alexandra, and the cat followed him out of curiosity since Alexandra and the cat had yet to see the bedchamber.

"Don't go near the big hole on the other side," the elf warned them as they approached the gigantic bed. The elf pulled the white drapes open on the side that faced the sinkhole and tied them together with the golden-tasseled ropes.

"Look at all this stuff!" Alexandra yelled upon seeing the mound of tributes.

Dame Logan removed her glasses to rub them with the sleeve of her robe, then put them back on, and squinted up. "Unbelievable!" she said.

The elf leaped into the bed and wobbled over to the skeleton of the king. There, he peeled the crown from the patchy skull and tossed it toward the black hole. The golden circle spun through the air and fell horizontally into the darkness without a sound. It was as if the darkness of the sink hole rose up to devour it.

With a loud whoop the elf reared back and kicked the skull as hard as he could toward the sinkhole. "Good riddance!" he yelled after it.

"No, wait!" Dame Logan shouted, her eyes round with fear.

But it was too late. As the skull flew nose over mouth over nose across the mound of candles and into the heat of their flames, which shimmered like the air over a copper roof on a hot afternoon, the hair on the skull burst into flames before it tumbled into the black hole. It was quiet for a long second while the scientist and the girl and the cat and the elf stared at the opening. Then a pillar of fire shot up from the sinkhole. The fire failed to spread to the edges of the floor. It looked as if the flames were sucked back down into the darkness with an enormous roar.

The elf certainly hadn't meant for that to happen and stood gaping.

"Everybody, run!" Dame Logan yelled and grabbed Alexandra's hand. The floor began to shake. A distant rumble rose up through the floor like an earthquake.

The elf picked up the cat, stuffed her inside his robe, and bounded after the scientist and her granddaughter toward the outer wall. There Dame Logan used a piece of fallen masonry to break the lower pane in a window. She pushed out the last shards with the stone and clambered up into the window. The elf helped Alexandra up and climbed after her.

"Stay low," Dame Logan said as they gazed down on the narrow ridge of lawn outside. Several large booms erupted from deep beneath them. The ground started to shake so much they couldn't have stayed in the window sill even if they had wanted to. They dropped down to the narrow ridge of lawn below. It was night, but the moon was up and shining so strongly it was easy to see the way.

"Hurry!" Dame Logan yelled and began to slide down the sloping garden toward the next terrace. "I just realized something!" she huffed as he ran. "And we don't want to be around when it happens!"

"Because the fire will spread from the hole to the catacombs?" the elf asked, grinning as he ran.

"No, worse!" Dame Logan shouted over the rumble. "To the sun!"

They ran and stumbled and fell and slid down the side of the castle-catacombs. Behind them the delicately arched windows and stained glass blew out into tinkling shards like the remains of the fallen chandelier they had passed in the hall of mirrors. Flames shot out of the ground—vertical yellow and orange pillars of fire. The ground shook so much it was almost impossible to run. Instead, they slid and skidded and rolled down the slopes.

WHEN THEY WERE almost down at the lawn-covered mother-of-pearl the ground trembled so violently they couldn't stand. The elf feared the top of the spiral was about to break off. They saw a plume of orange flames burst out of the tip of the shell's spire and up into Spiral's sun. The golden orb exploded in an enormous, deafening, blinding ball of fire.

"Ahh!" the elf screamed, but inside he was howling with laughter. Had he known that kicking the king's head into the sinkhole would have had this effect, he would have done it much sooner.

"Ooh!" Dame Logan gasped, but her eyes were bright and full of hope.

"Magnificent," Alexandra huffed as they fled down toward the rest of Spiral.

ELEVEN
GOING HOME

WITH THE ARTIFICIAL SUN GONE AND the delivery of the royal message to the Academy from the Guardsman, Dame Logan's theorem was accepted and added to the official records of the Academic Tier. It was decreed that the Earth orbited the sun and not the other way around. Dame Logan was invited to present her discovery in the foyer of the Academy as her reinstatement lecture. It turned out that no one had died in the fire in the lecture hall and all the spheres for the planetary model had been saved from the ashes.

The elf was acquitted of the accusation of arson since the fire had been an accident and several scholars could attest to that, but he was nevertheless asked to leave the city due to his negligence of safety precautions. Dame Logan wisely never mentioned the other, bigger accident to anyone, and the rest of the city gained news of the exploded sun from the bang itself. When it started raining bones and skulls all over Spiral, Guards and Scholars sent a team to investigate what had happened in the noble tier. The investigative team found what was left of the royal bedchamber, the hill of tributes, and the great lie. The rumors from their findings were unstoppable, and for some time it looked as if a struggle of power between the Guardians, the Scholars, and the Merchants would break out.

Severely weakened and being a considerable hazard for the tier below it, the last remaining clamp holding the Prison Cellar to the mother-of-pearl was loosened. With a graceful tumble and spin the jail fell into the bay, filled slowly with water as if it actively resisted its fate, and sank without a trace in the dark water.

Fortunately for the city, the illness turned out to be much less contagious than initially feared. It had not grown strong enough to be able to jump from human to human, and so it stopped with the people who had been infected by the mud drops in the air. A tally performed by some scholars showed that it was indeed the noble tier that had taken the worst toll. No survivors were found in the castle-catacombs because of the necessity there of keeping the windows open due to the charnel stench no matter the weather and because many nobles had been outside to duel and joust in the dramatic weather.

The Guardian tier also lost many who had been patrolling the streets during the storm. Thus, the upper tiers were so weakened that they had to ally with the Scholar and Merchant tiers. A league of tiers was created instead, modeled after the merchant houses in Canal, and set to rule the city and its region.

Before the elf left Spiral he snuck into the party that celebrated Dame Logan's re-inauguration to the Academy of Natural Sciences.

"Please return to Spiral after a while when the ruckus has calmed down," Dame Logan said. " I regard you as one of my apprentices, although not the safest one. Alexandra is about to continue her studies as well."

The elf bowed deeply to her—not with one of his sardonic, exaggerated bows, but a simple and honest one. It was the first bow he had done for a long time and actually meant it. "I would love to, but I can't," he said. "I realize that the academic life is not for me. I'm a wanderer."

Dame Logan nodded but wiped the corner of her eye. "I guess you're right," she said. "At least know that, when you return to Spiral, you have a home with me."

"I thank you, Scholar," the elf said. "And I thank you for traveling and tolerating me for so long during our journeys."

Dame Logan laughed. "It was close a few times. But it all turned out good in the end. Not just for us, but for the entire city."

Outside the Academy of Natural Sciences, the elf hugged Dame Logan and Alexandra and mounted his horse. This time a proper horse instead of a cat. The cat sat on the elf's shoulder and was ready to go home, too.

When the cat and elf finally returned to the cold shores they had left so long ago it was still summer, and the endless sun filled the air with a golden glow.

"Can you feel that? We're home now," the elf said.

The cat peeked out and sniffed the air, her dark snout

vibrating. "I can!" she meowed. "Finally!" She dug her claws into the skin on the elf's chest.

The meadow along the shore was in full flower. They dismounted the horse. The brown creature whinnied, then ran off into the field, hooves kicking and tail whipping. Then it lay down and rolled its back and sides in the green grass.

The cat sniffed and headbutted the flowers and purred and chased the bumblebees and butterflies for a while. Afterwards, she returned to the elf, who patted her back and head like he always did.

"Are you going back to the sea?" the cat asked.

"That was the plan," the elf said and gazed out on the still water that glimmered in the midnight sun.

"Are you certain you don't want to stay a little?" the cat said. "The hut can be repaired—it's not that run down—and the eider ducks will be leaving soon. We can line the walls with down, and there's peat in the marsh to burn for the winter."

She pushed against the elf's hands some more.

"You just want a warm belly to sleep on and hands to light the fireplace when the cold gets here," the elf said.

"Meow," said the cat. "But I enjoy your company, too."

The elf stood and stretched and smiled into the warm evening. The midnight sun warmed his face and hands, and the mild breeze carried the scent of ocean and heather and flowering meadow. "I suppose I can stay a little longer," the elf said, smiling, and pet the cat some more.

About the Author

Berit Ellingsen is the author of three novels, *Now We Can See The Moon* (Snuggly Books 2018), *Not Dark Yet* (Two Dollar Radio 2015), and *Une ville vide* (PublieMonde 2014), a collection of short stories, *Beneath the Liquid Skin* (Queen's Ferry Press), and a mini-collection of dark fairy-tales, *Vessel and Solsvart* (Snuggly Books 2017). Her work has been published in *W.W. Norton's Flash Fiction International, SmokeLong Quarterly, Unstuck, Litro, Lightspeed*, and other places, and has been nominated for the Pushcart Prize, Best of the Net, and the British Science Fiction Association Award. Berit is a member of the Norwegian Authors' Union. You can follow Berit at beritellingsen.com